MISTER IRRESISTIBLE

BACHELOR INTERNATIONAL BOOK 2

TARA SUE ME

After Six Publishing

ISBN Ebook: 9781950017263

ISBN Print: 9781950017294

Cover image: Deposit Photos

She came into my arms willingly, and for one perfect second, all was right in my world. Emotions I'd never experienced and had no name for consumed me. My only path of action was to release those emotions on her.

I tightened my arms around her; deepened our kiss. She moaned in reply.

What would it be like to have this every day? Could my body even function under such bliss? I wasn't sure, but vowed to do everything in my power to make us happen.

I assumed her thoughts ran in parallel to mine, but at once I sensed a hesitancy in her that hadn't been there seconds before.

Damn it all. I would not lose her again.
I didn't care what I had to do.

CHAPTER 1

WREN

My best friend, Mia, was up to something. That was the only reason I could think of to explain why she'd ask if I wanted to do dinner after work.

Don't get me wrong, I loved her, and she'd been my best friend for as long as I could remember, but ever since she got together with Tenor Butler two months ago, I hadn't seen much of her. Not that I blamed her. She was madly in love and wanted to spend every waking minute with her man. And by every waking minute, I meant that literally. They lived and worked together.

The three of us had been out a few times, but I didn't enjoy being the third wheel, and no matter how nice Tenor was, there was no escaping the fact that I was the odd man out. Just like those puzzles I used to do in elementary school, the ones where you had to pick out which thing didn't belong? Circle me with the red crayon, you found it.

Mia and I had just received our vegan taco order from one of our favorite restaurants, and were making our way to an empty table outside.

"This one?" She pointed with her free hand. "It's mostly shade."

"Works for me." I sat down and she followed.

"What? Why are you staring at me?"

"Tell me what's going on," I said and took a bite of my taco, tired of waiting for her to spit out the reason she asked me to dinner.

"What makes you think anything is going on?" she asked, and her voice sounded so by-your-leave if I hadn't known her forever, she might have fooled me.

I rolled my eyes. "Because you've been up Tenor's butt lately. Granted, it's a nice-looking butt, and I can see the appeal, but the two of us haven't been out to dinner alone in over two months."

She stopped chewing and swallowed before answering. "It hasn't been that long."

I raised an eyebrow.

"Has it?" she asked.

"I get it," I said. "I do. But I still think something's going on."

Fortunately, she didn't even try to say otherwise. "You remember the match questionnaire you filled out for me about a month ago?"

Mia and Tenor co-owned a matchmaking business, Bachelor International. The company was the most successful of its type in Boston before Mia joined, and after she did, they're nearing the top of agencies on the east coast. Especially since a satellite office recently opened in Atlanta. Mia and Tenor have been working to update the questions they ask new clients, and Mia asked me to fill out one of their new questionnaires because they needed more data points.

"Yes," I said. "What about it?"

"You filled it out with truthful information, right? You didn't make stuff up because it was something I asked you to do?" She took a bite of taco and waited for my response.

To be quite honest, I'd thought about filling it out with completely ridiculous answers, but ended up being truthful. After all, the data points wouldn't be helpful if they were all outliers.

"I filled it out with truthful answers," I said, and then narrowed my eyes. "Why do you ask?"

Mia put her taco down on her plate, and that's when I knew she meant business. Putting food down meant she didn't want any distractions while she spoke. I had the sudden urge to run screaming from the table.

"An international client has hired us for his upcoming visit to the States," she said. Nothing new there. I mean, seriously, the business was called Bachelor International. One would assume they got similar requests all the time. I didn't see what any of it had to do with me.

"Anyway," Mia continued. "Tenor asked if I thought you'd be a suitable match for this guy. Of course, I couldn't say definitively one way or another unless I compared your answers with his. So I did, and Wren, you're the best match out of our entire database."

My brain tried to stop listening as soon as it heard, "Tenor asked if I thought you'd be a suitable match for this guy," but somehow I managed to hang on until the end.

"And what?" I asked. "You want to pair me up with him? Why? I'm not a client of yours." Not to mention I wasn't looking for a relationship and had no interest in being matched with a snotty international who more than likely had more money than God. I didn't care what her database thought.

"You're not interested at all?" she asked. "Don't you want to know even a little about him? Doesn't the fact that you match him better than all the other women we have in our database intrigue you just a bit?"

I laughed. "How many is that? Twenty? It can't be that many or else you wouldn't have needed more data points."

She didn't reply, but picked her taco up and took another bite.

I waited.

She took another bite.

The truth hit me all at once, and I groaned. How could I have been so stupid? "You didn't need my answers for data points, did you?" I didn't have to wait for her answer. Why would an agency as large and as successful as Bachelor International need my data points?

They didn't.

"I didn't need your answers for data points, per se," Mia confessed. "I may have stretched the truth a bit."

"Why did you need them?" I asked, but she didn't answer. "Mia?"

"I needed them to match you, and I knew you'd stay no if I told you that. So yes, I may have stretched the truth, but it was only because I'm worried about you."

"Worried about me, why?" I shook my head. "You could have just asked if I wanted to be in your database."

She hadn't, though, because she knew I'd have told her no way.

"You wouldn't have filled it out if I told you it was for real," she said.

"And?" I asked. "You think this way is better?"

"Yes, I do, actually," she said. "I found you a near perfect match, and all you have to do is show up for dinner."

I snorted. "That's all I have to do?"

"Come on, Wren," she said. "When was the last time you went out with a guy? For a real date?"

I shot her a glare. She knew exactly how long it'd been. What's more, I'd finally told her why it'd been that long a few months ago. "You know when the last time was."

"And you're never going to move on if you don't put yourself out there, and at least try."

"Maybe I don't want to move on," I said, cringing at hearing how ridiculous my reply sounded. I knew that wasn't what I really wanted. It's just that it was easier to go about my life not putting myself out there very much. After a year or two, it became my routine. Staying at home was easier than going out. Boring and predictable, yes. I'd even go so far as to say mildly pathetic. But it was mine, and it was comfortable.

"If that's the case," Mia said. "Then no big deal. I'll get in contact with his second match, and that will be that."

I hated it when she called my bluff. Because regardless of what I or anyone else thought of my life, I really didn't want it to stay the way it was forever. To be honest, I didn't know how to do anything differently. I hated the singles scene, and couldn't afford a professional like Bachelor International.

Then maybe you should take Mia up on her offer, I told myself. "When did you say this guy was coming into town, and when am I supposed to meet him?"

Mia did a horrible job hiding her grin, which just proved my point about her calling my bluff. She'd known the entire time, and I had played right into her hands. "There's an event he has next Saturday."

"What kind of event?" I asked.

"A reception and dinner, I believe."

"I'm not going to meet him before the event?"

"No," she said, but didn't expand.

"Why is this sounding more like an escort service than a matchmaking one?" I asked.

Mia's mouth dropped open in shock. "You know I'd have nothing to do with an escort service."

"I know," I said. "But you have to admit, it sounds a bit odd."

"Not odd," Mia corrected me. "It's what the client asked for. He needs a date for the event and wanted someone he would more than likely get along with. He's coming into town the day of the event, so there's no time for a date before then."

"Flying internationally into Boston the day of an event makes no sense." It boggled the mind. "Doesn't he have people who tell him stuff like that is stupid as hell?"

"I'm sure he does, but he's not flying in from an international location. He'll be in New York for a few days, and then he'll fly to Boston."

I'd be lying to say part of me wasn't interested in getting all glammed up for a night out. I couldn't remember the last time I'd done so. Even if I had to put up with a snooty international who had more money than God. Maybe this would be the kick in the butt I needed to get my social life breathing again.

"I'll think about it," I said to Mia. She probably knew I was going to end up agreeing to do it anyway and only dragged it out to give her grief.

Either way, her face lit up like she'd just spied Tenor standing behind me. "That's all I ask," she said. "And that you let me know by Monday morning one way or the other."

"Today's Wednesday," I said. "That'll never work because if I decide to go, I'll need something new to wear, and you and I will have to go shopping. The best time for me to go is Saturday morning. Let Tenor know now so that he can come to terms with not spending time with you for a few hours on Saturday."

Mia held a hand up to her mouth. "We're not that bad, are we?"

I narrowed my gaze. "Two months."

Mia only smiled. "They've flown by."

I didn't have it in my heart to pick on her too much. She'd been through a lot in the last year and truly deserved her chance at happiness. I'd never deny her that. After losing both a friend and her mother in a car crash, she'd then lost her business only a few weeks later. Even though she hooked up with Tenor soon thereafter, they had a huge misunderstanding, and went weeks without seeing each other.

"I'm so happy with Tenor," she said. "I never thought I'd feel this way about anyone. Much less him. I mean, I disliked him from the second I heard of him."

"I think the word you're looking for there is hate, not dislike," I felt necessary to remind her. Before meeting Tenor in person, Mia's disdain for anything remotely related to either Tenor or Bachelor International was legendary.

She nodded and looked at me directly. "I was so wrong about him, but the one thing I did right was not to let my preconceived ideas of who he was cloud my ability to let me see the real man."

"This feels like you're trying to fit an after-school special in there somewhere, but I'm totally missing whatever it is."

"I'm saying you had an awful experience with a guy in the past. Don't let that one experience control you to where it ruins your perception of all men." Mia took a sip of water. "I believe there are a lot of good guys out there."

"And that, my friend, is why you're the matchmaker and I'm the coldhearted journalist."

"Please. You don't have a cold heart."

"Cold and dead," I insisted.

"I don't believe you for a second," Mia said. "It might be a bit on the frosty side, but all it needs is the right man to thaw it."

I snorted. "Whatever. Tell me what you can about this guy."

Mia's eyes blazed with victory and I held up my hand. "Don't get excited. I'm not saying I'll do it, I'm saying tell me a little about him, and I'll think on it tonight and let you know definitively tomorrow."

"He's Italian—"

"Wait. What?"

Mia looked unsure for the first time since bringing up the entire date. "That's the reason Tenor brought up your name for a potential date in the first place. He thought since you'd spent time in Italy, you'd be perfect."

My time in Italy was the reason why I had a heart so cold and dead. A fact I had only recently confided to Mia. "Does he know...?" I found myself unable to finish the question.

"No, Wren," she assured me. "Of course not. I would never betray your trust in such a way. Not even to Tenor."

Not that I thought she would, but I had to be certain and didn't feel bad at all for asking. I took a deep breath, forcing the air out of my lungs before inhaling. I could do this. Hell, it'd been years, and in that time, I'd become an expert at shutting that part of myself away, not only from the world, but from myself as well. "Okay, so he's Italian. What else?"

She didn't look half as assured as she had been only seconds before, but she continued. "His name is Lucrezio, and he's in the US for marketing of some sort. He's two years older than you and has never been married."

A businessman from Italy. I took another deep breath. "Anything else?"

"Other than the fact he's a perfect match?"

"What did the background check show?" I knew before accepting any client, Bachelor International always ran a background check. According to Mia, they'd found nothing while doing a background check that would disqualify someone from being a client, but they wouldn't take a chance and not do one.

"His background was relatively unremarkable. Close friends describe him as a workaholic, very driven, and somewhat reclusive."

He sounded dreadfully boring. Since boring wasn't a word I'd have used to describe my time in Italy, or my experience with Italian men, I let myself relax. I could do this. "I'll think about it tonight," I told Mia. "And let you know something tomorrow."

BEFORE MY TIME IN ITALY, I scoffed at the idea of love at first sight. Foolishness, I'd say with a shake of my head at how supposedly intelligent people could lower their intellect enough to believe in such nonsense.

But then I went to Italy for two weeks.

It had never been my plan to travel abroad that year. If I'd even considered it for longer than two seconds, I'd have decided fairly quickly the cost would be outside anything I'd be able to pay. At the time, I was going to school part time, while working as a ballet instructor. My dream was to become a professional dancer, and any free time I had outside of school was spent doing some sort of dance, usually ballet.

A group of friends I'd met in school arranged a ski trip to Italy over Christmas break. They'd asked if I was interested. Of course, I'd said. But being interested and being able to afford the trip were two different things.

My parents had moved to Florida when they retired and had announced earlier that October they'd booked a Christmas cruise when they found a bargain last minute deal online. Since they lived near Miami, they could take a cab to the port.

I'd planned to spend the holidays with Mia and her mom, and was looking forward to catching up with Mia. Between her job and my schedule, we'd have very little girl bonding time. I didn't even mind being around her mom. Dee was like a second mom to me, but a really cool second mom. Italy never crossed my mind as a possibility until three weeks before the group was due to leave, one of the travelers was arrested for accessory to armed robbery and wasn't allowed to leave the country.

Because of the way the package the group had purchased worked, the entire trip would be cancelled if they were unable to fill that empty spot. When they called to ask if I could go, I still thought it could never happen, until they convinced me to talk to the travel agent, and she quoted me a price I'd be a fool not to take.

Fortunately, I had a passport, and after some whirlwind shopping, a few weeks later I was on my way to Italy. I flew out of Boston feeling as if I was on top of the world. I had to pinch myself to make sure it wasn't a dream.

The resort in Courmayeur, Italy was more beautiful than I had ever imagined a place could be. When I met Luca the day I arrived, I allowed myself to get swept away by his soulful eyes, his good looks, and easy charm, but most of all, his sweet words. For the best ten days of my life, I thought my initial belief about love at first sight was a mistake on my part. After all, Luca and I had fallen that quickly.

But a little over a week was all it lasted. Ten days. Ten days were all I had to experience the type of love I never believed possible. Ten days before it was ripped from my hands and shown to be sham it was. Ten days before I lost not only the man I thought was my soulmate and the love of my life, but also, my forever dream of dance. With one foolish mistake, I lost everything.

CHAPTER 2

LUCA

"I've checked you into your suite at the Boston Harbor Hotel, Mr. Botticelli," my personal assistant, Carmella, informed me as the private jet I'd booked for the short flight from New York City prepared to land.

She continued to talk, reminding me of my schedule for what felt like the hundredth time. I knew exactly what my schedule was and how busy I'd be for the short time I'd be in Boston. At least for this trip. Deciding to move my business overseas from Italy to the US wouldn't be taken care of in the span of a week.

Carmella continued to talk, and I all but tuned her out. She didn't mind flying, but landing always made her nervous. One way she dealt with her unease was to ramble. Which was fine, I mean we all have our idiosyncrasies, right? But that didn't mean I had to listen to her.

I did, however, catch the name she dropped, not having remembered her mentioning it before. "What was that one?"

She looked up in shock. I normally let her ramble uninterrupted, so I'd obviously caught her off guard by questioning her.

"What was what one?" she asked.

"Who wants to meet sometime between now and the reception?" I asked. "And when did you schedule them?"

"Tenor Butler, sir," she said. "And I thought maybe he could come up and wait in the sitting area. I think that's the best way for you to get together before you meet your date."

"He didn't say what he wanted to discuss?"

"No, sir," she said, and when I didn't reply, she started going through tomorrow's schedule, allowing me to once more tune her out. It was bothersome that Tenor wanted to discuss something before the reception. Maybe my date had backed out.

I chuckled. No way would I be that lucky.

The truth was, I didn't want to go with anyone to the reception tonight. Hell, if I'd had my way, I wouldn't be going. But it was an annual fundraiser for the East Coast Fashion Designer's Association and as a new fashion designer, in the States anyway, it would behoove me to show up. And according to my board of advisors, I needed to have a date.

Funny, if you'd have told me five years ago, that there would come a time when I'd rather spend the evening alone than in the company of a woman, I'd have laughed my ass off. Five years ago, I usually went out with a different woman every night, and didn't think a thing of it. But all that had been before my little bird flew in and out of my life so quickly at times I still wonder if I dreamt her up.

The pain she left in my heart, however, was a stark reminder of how real she'd been. I kept my feelings about her to myself, very few people knew of her. Most of those in my acquaintance thought it was something else entirely that completely changed my world that week.

To this day, I can't say exactly what drew the two of us together in such a quick and intense manner. Logically, I should have discounted our connection as mere hormones, but when my grandparents were alive, they loved to tell anyone who would listen about how they knew they were destined to be together from the moment their eyes first met. When you grow up listening to that, while you may not believe it'll ever happen to you, you recognize it for what it is when it does.

That's what it had been like when I met Wren.

And for ten days, damn near everything was perfect.

I'm not sure what drove her away, or why, when she ran, she ran so hard and fast. I knew there had been a ski accident, and she was hurt. She wouldn't allow anyone to visit her, and as soon as she could leave, she was gone. And just like that, my little bird flew out of my life as quickly as she'd flown in.

We hadn't exchanged phone numbers or email addresses. Why should we have? In our minds, or at least mine, we had plenty of time to deal with such trivial things. She had never given me her family name, nor did I give her mine.

I'm still stunned at how quickly all the time I thought we had disappeared in a second. I talked with several people in the days following her accident, those that travel from the US with her, as well as those who were at the ski resort with me. No one could agree on what happened or why Wren was so insistent that she didn't want to see me.

"Mr. Botticelli?" Carmella asked, and I realized we had landed and the flight crew was waiting for us to disembark.

"Apologies," I said, standing and grabbing my carry-on.

Carmella gave me a sad smile. She'd started working for me right before I met Wren. As such, she knew about her and was also aware that at the time of her visit, Wren lived in Boston.

"More than likely she doesn't live here anymore," Carmella said after we were off the plane and waiting for our driver to load our luggage into the car.

I wasn't a fool, I knew Boston was a large city, and that even if Wren still happened to live in the area, the odds weren't likely of our paths crossing. But the fact that I was so transparent to Carmella bothered me.

The driver walked to the side of the car and opened the back door. I waited until Carmella made it inside before climbing in and taking my seat beside her.

"I don't know what you're talking about," I lied, thankful I'd kept my sunglasses on so she couldn't see my eyes and recognize the lie I'd just told. Even still, I was pretty sure she didn't believe me.

A FEW HOURS LATER, I was dressed for the reception and opened the door to the suite's sitting room where Tenor Butler waited. We'd only exchanged emails mostly, though I had spoken with him a few times. He seemed to me more of a business executive than someone who worked and owned a match maker company. Of course, maybe that was why Bachelor International was so successful.

He turned from the large picture window he'd been standing in front of and walked to meet me.

"Tenor Butler," he said. "Nice to meet you."

I shook his hand. "Lucrezio Botticelli. I go by Luca." I waved him toward the semicircle of couches in the middle of the room. "The request for the meeting caught me off guard. Is something wrong?"

"No," Tenor said. "I try to meet all our international clients face-to-face before their first date."

I nodded, there were several reasons I could think of for him to do so. Everything from client safety to customer service.

He chuckled. "When I called Ms. Marino to set up a time to meet with you, she assumed the same thing. Told me it wouldn't be an issue if that was the case, because she had no problem filling in and being your date for the evening."

Of course she wouldn't, I thought, but kept to myself. Carmela made no secret of the fact that she wished to be more than my personal assistant. It would never happen because of a long list of reasons, only one of those reasons being that she worked for me. As a personal assistant, she was the best I'd ever had. She was organized, thorough, and had an uncanny ability to anticipate what I needed before I realized I needed it.

However, outside of the office, she had a tendency to speak without a filter and to act without appearing to think about what she was doing beforehand. I had never figured out what the deal was, why she seemed to have two distinct personalities. I didn't let it bother me, or to use much brain power trying to understand. As long as she continued to do her job the way she'd been doing it, she could keep her Dr. Jekyll and Mr. Hyde moments. As long as she kept them away from me.

But even that wasn't the primary reason. I sighed, knowing I couldn't think about the primary reason at the moment.

"That doesn't surprise me," I told Tenor, resisting the temptation to run my hand through my hair.

He nodded, giving me the impression he knew exactly what I was talking about. "Did you have any questions about the process or the woman we've matched you with?"

While I was in New York City, Tenor's business partner, Mia, had sent me a long email containing what I assumed were details on my date for the evening. I hadn't bothered to read it, but felt somewhat guilty admitting as much sitting with Tenor the way I was.

I simply replied, "No, no questions at all." That sounded better than telling the truth which was reading the details of the woman I'd be meeting wouldn't change anything about how the date would go or how it would end. I needed a date for the event tonight and didn't want to use an escort service. Signing up with a matchmaker sounded a lot more practical.

I had a plan for the evening. I'd be standoffish enough that my date wouldn't consider thinking twice about another date with me. Of course, I'd be a gentleman, it's who I was, and I wouldn't do anything to sully my reputation. I could live with my date calling me a bore after tonight, but I wouldn't go so far as to be considered an asshole.

That was the plan, anyway.

"Have you had the chance to look into a place to live?" Tenor asked.

"I have," I told him truthfully, assuming he was just making small talk in an effort to get to know me better. "But I'm interested in getting your take on the different neighborhoods."

"I'm a bit partial to this area," he said. "Mia and I have been talking about looking for a place here near the water. Right now we're in a townhouse closer to the city center."

I hadn't realized he was living with his business partner. Not that it mattered. I only thought it was interesting.

"You have to admit," he said, standing and walking back toward the large picture window. "This is an incredible view."

I made the appropriate noises, because I stopped noticing things like beautiful views around the time Wren left. Not that I couldn't see the beauty, it was more that I didn't notice it until someone pointed it out. Looking out the window that Tenor indicated, I had to agree. The view of the Back Bay was quite lovely.

"Maybe we'll be neighbors then," I said. "If I end up feeling the same."

I couldn't help but to glance back at the water. I'd bet it was even more incredible at night with lights bouncing off of the surface.

"Sounds good," he said, and turned away from the window back toward me. "I've taken up enough of your time. I'll take my leave and let you finish up before heading to the reception. I hope the night exceeds all your expectations."

"Nice meeting you, Tenor," I called out as he left. I didn't add that my expectations were so low, it'd take a massive disaster to not meet them.

Still not entirely sure why he wanted to meet, I went back to the bedroom of the suite to take one last look in the mirror to make sure I looked decent. Good enough.

A glance at my watch told me I still had about forty minutes until I was to meet my date in the lobby. I tucked the purple flower in my jacket pocket. Mia had it waiting for me in the room when I arrived with a note informing me it would allow my date to recognize me. Completely ready, I stopped by the bar for a quick drink before heading to the lobby.

CHAPTER 3

WREN

"Here he comes," Mia said, with a nod toward the window, and I glanced over to see Tenor crossing the street.

We were sitting in a coffee shop across from the hotel Lucrezio was staying at, which was also where the reception and dinner would be held. It had been Mia's idea for Tenor to set up a meeting with my so-called match in the hopes that he'd be able to do away with any fears I might have about going out with a stranger. I'd told her it was unnecessary, but she wouldn't listen. And then Tenor chimed in saying he thought it was a good idea as well.

After that, I knew I could hang it up. Arguing with one of them about anything to do with Bachelor International was bad enough, but pair them together and you could forget about it.

"He doesn't look very happy, does he?" I asked Mia.

Her lips were pressed tightly together. Obviously, she felt the same, but she refused to admit as much. "That's his thinking face."

"Looks more like an *I have to get Wren out of this ASAP* face to me," I mumbled under my breath.

Mia wisely pretended like she didn't hear me and didn't speak again until Tenor made his way to our table.

He sat down beside Mia with a sigh.

"What?" Mia asked.

He raised an eyebrow at her. "You mean to tell me using your method of matching, Wren was that guy's highest match?"

My heart jumped up to my throat. "Why? Is he a serial killer or something?"

Mia tried to cover her shock. "I know you're joking. I've used that method for years and have hundreds of happy matches."

But Tenor didn't look like he was joking. "I think it's wrong this time. No, he's not a serial killer, though maybe if he was, he'd have a better personality."

"What's that supposed to mean?" I asked.

Tenor winced as he looked at me. "That guy is boring as hell. Zero personality and walks like he has a stick up his ass."

His answer was so different from what I'd expected based on his expression when he walked in, I couldn't help it, I laughed.

"I don't believe it," Mia said. "There's no way she could match so well with either a bore or a serial killer. Maybe he just didn't like you."

Tenor ignored her. "Wren, I'm sorry you got matched with such a bore. Try not to fall asleep. Leave early if you want to, and Mia and I will make it up to you."

Mia crossed her arms and shot him the evil eye before focusing on me. "If you need a rescue, text me the letter z and I'll call and give you an out. Don't lose hope just yet. It's possible he didn't like Tenor, or he was just tired. The guy has been traveling a lot."

"Everyone likes me," Tenor said with a grin. "Didn't you get the memo? Odds are he's a dud."

I shrugged. It wasn't like I had high hopes for the night, anyway. "At least I got a nice dress out of it."

"It's an awesome dress," Mia countered.

It was an awesome dress. Mia and I had gone shopping over the past weekend, and had lucked out and found a high-dollar department store having a closeout sale. The navy blue gown didn't look like much of anything on the rack, which is probably why it was unsold, but once I put it on, I knew I had to have it. I loved everything about gown. The delicate halter neck. The way the fabric gently hugged my curves in all the right places without making me feel as if I couldn't breathe. The long, flowy fabric covering my legs. The blue hue that brought out the color of my eyes. Every inch of it was perfect and made me feel like a hundred bucks when I had it on.

"If you have to be bored out of your mind, at least you'll look good doing it," Tenor said. "Ow," he added, which I assumed meant Mia kicked him under the table.

"Want us to walk with you?" Mia asked.

"No." I stood up. It was time for me to leave if I wanted to arrive a minute or two early. "It's just across the street."

Mia slipped out of her chair and gave me a hug. "You look fabulous. I hope you have an amazing night, but remember to text me if you need an out."

"I think I can handle being bored for a few hours." If I stuck it out, maybe Mia would stop telling me how I needed to get out more. And if she brought up the subject, I could easily reply that I had been out with a man she matched me with, and that the experience was enough to last me for at least a year.

I hadn't taken very many steps when I heard Mia ask Tenor, "He really wasn't that bad, was he?"

Tenor laughed, and if he answered, I missed it by stepping outside.

The sun had started its descent, but though it was still light, the air held a slight chill, as if reminding us autumn was just around the corner. Not that many of us who'd ever spent a winter in Boston could forget. I loved my city, but I hated the winters. Especially since Italy. While once upon a time I'd found the freshly fallen snow beautiful; now I only saw it as the catalyst in the series of reactions that landed me where I was - alone and unable to dance.

I crossed the road, telling myself to snap out of it. Even if my date turned out to be duller than an unsharpened pencil, I was going to give him a chance and not walk into the lobby with my mind made up about him before we actually met. Nor did I want to come across as a morose woman living in the past.

I caught sight of myself in the glass of a nearby building and almost didn't recognize my reflection. With my dark blond hair styled and pulled into a delicate updo, makeup applied, and wearing something other than the baggy jeans and ratty tee shirts that made up most of my work-from-home wardrobe, I didn't look half bad. I stood up a bit straighter and squared my shoulders. Totally unlike me, but damn it, I looked good, and I was going to own that shit.

The lobby of the hotel was crowded with other beautiful people, most of them paired off, but there were a few groups and a handful of singles. Mia had told me Lucrezio would be wearing a purple flower in his lapel. I'd giggled when she first told me how Bachelor International clients did so when they needed a quick way to be identified. Now, however, it made complete sense.

Had I not been told to look for a man with a purple flower, I couldn't imagine how awkward it would be to try to figure out who my date was. I tried to picture myself attempting to decide which men looked the most like the Italian men I'd met before, and then what? Go up to each of them and ask, "Are you my date?" That would never happen, no matter how good I looked. One second of that, and I'd be on the way back home alone.

Thankfully, that wasn't the case. I took a quick look around the lobby. But none of the men present had any sort of flower in their lapel. There were a few single men at the bar off in the far corner of the lobby, but I didn't want to walk in that direction, since we'd agreed to meet in the lobby. Besides, I was a few minutes early, it wasn't as if I was being stood up. I tried not to think about how embarrassing that would be and settled instead on people watching while looking for lapels filled with flowers.

What I ended up doing was keeping my eyes open for a lapel flower while wondering what my boss would think of an investigative article on being stood up by the world's biggest bore.

Since my focus was on flowers, that's what I noticed first. One of the single men at the bar left and started walking toward the lobby. As soon as he turned my direction, I saw the purple flower in his lapel. I found myself unable to look away from the flower, though I wasn't sure why. Was I really that surprised he showed up?

It wasn't until he'd almost reached me that I lifted my gaze to see his face and ended up meeting his eyes. Eyes I'd never forget.

I let out a gasp as the world tilted and everything went black.

CHAPTER 4

WREN

5 years ago

I WAS STARTING to think the Italy trip was a mistake. Pretty sad since I hadn't been in the country for even twenty-four hours. We'd landed, made our way through customs, and were currently in a shared van on our way to the resort we were staying at. I'd never felt so out of place in my life.

It was becoming crystal clear the members of my travel group were more interested in parties and who was going to be at them, than they were with skiing or even seeing the Italian countryside. I'm not sure why this surprised me because they did the same thing at home. Silly me for thinking they'd act any different in a foreign country.

By the time we pulled up to the resort, I'd already come to terms with the fact I'd pretty much be on my own for the entire trip. Good thing I never had a problem being in my own company. It appeared the group felt the same way about me. No one seemed to be in a hurry to invite me along to any parties. Not that I cared, but it would have been nice to have at least been invited.

I stood in the lobby with everyone else, waiting while the two group leaders, Laura and Betsy, went to check everyone in. The rooms were double, and that was the part I dreaded. Who would I be sharing a room with?

Everything must have been ready because in no time at all, we were being given room assignments. I held my breath. When Laura was down to one passcard, she looked at me. "They upgraded Betsy and me to a suite, and since we have so much room, Michelle's going to room with us. You don't mind having a room all to yourself, do you?"

Obviously, Michelle had drawn the short stick and yet somehow could still twist it in such a way as to make it work for her. Just as well. She had a shrill laugh guaranteed to give me a headache in under two point five seconds. At least I wouldn't have to hear that all day, every day the entire time we were here.

"No, of course not," I said.

With that settled to everyone's satisfaction, the group turned and left for the elevators, leaving their luggage for the porter to bring later. They'd all brought more bags than they could possibly need. I'd only packed a carry-on and a checked bag. Of course, I wasn't planning to change outfits five times a day, either.

I didn't want to ride the elevator with them, especially since I planned to carry my own bags, so I purposely slowed down. Laura actually took the time to glance over her shoulder and asked, "Are you coming?"

I waved her on. Not in your life. "I need to check with the concierge really quick. I'll be right up."

She gave me a little smile and turned back to the group. Their laughter lingered behind them as they walked away. I watched until they disappeared around a corner. Maybe I should have been bothered, but I wasn't. I was in Italy for Christmas, at a beautiful resort, with days of doing whatever I wanted. It might not be the perfect scenario, but I wasn't about to complain about it.

Letting out a deep sigh, I reached for the handle of my bag, and somehow knocked it over. This shouldn't have been a problem, and it wouldn't have been if I hadn't placed my purse on top of my bag, propped up against the pull handle. Even that shouldn't have been an issue. Except my purse was open.

So there I was in the middle of this gorgeous and elegant lobby set in a resort in the Italian Alps, and I'd just scattered the contents of my purse across the lobby. And because I crammed it full of stuff I thought I might need on the plane, there were tubes of lip balm, hand lotion, hand sanitizer, wet wipes, a half-filled bottle of water, and assorted nuts and dried berries decorating the floor at my feet.

For a moment I stared at the mess, mortified, before I scrambled to my knees, hurriedly trying to pick everything up before it had a chance to escape further. I managed to gather everything up without it getting stepped on and dumped the pile into my purse. I was certain I looked like a hot mess, but the marble floor must be kept fastidiously clean because my jeans were dust free when I went to brush them off. Still feeling like everyone in the lobby was staring at me, even though I could see that they weren't, I picked the sanitizer out of my purse and cleaned my hands.

Finished, I ensured all my bags were closed properly and zipped up.

"Excuse me," a deep, accented voice said from behind me. "I think this is yours."

Turning, I found myself staring at what had to be the finest male specimen to ever walk the face of the earth. I was pretty certain he could serve as the example of what a tall, dark, and handsome man should look like.

I realized I'd been staring at him for longer than what was polite when he smiled and said, "It might not be yours, but I thought I'd ask."

Glancing down to see what it was, I wanted to crawl into a hole when I did. Because Mr. Hotter-than-any-man-has-a-right-to-be was holding the small travel bag I used for tampons. My face heated, and I didn't need a mirror to tell me my cheeks were red. Irritated at how my body reacted to him, I snatched the tampons out of his grip. I probably wouldn't need them and had thrown them in my purse at the last second.

I'd often wondered later what would have happened if I'd decided not to pack the tampons? Would Luca and I have never met, or would he have found something else to pick up that day? Maybe we wouldn't have met in the lobby shortly after my arrival, but rather later in the week having coffee in front of one of the enormous public rooms the resort had. Then I'd think, if we hadn't met until later, would I have fallen so far, so fast? Would the accident that forever altered the course of my life not have happened?

Could a travel bag filled with tampons really have such an immense influence on your life's path?

It boggled the mind.

Of course, at that point in time, I knew nothing of what the next week would bring. All I knew was that a hot Italian guy was holding my tampons.

"Yes, it is mine. Thank you," I said, and he laughed.

"I see you've only arrived just now," he said.

"Very astute," I said, not understanding why I was acting so pissy to the hot guy. He was only being nice by picking up something I'd dropped. It wasn't his fault I was embarrassed he'd found my tampons.

"Jet lag can be a pain in the ass," he said, seeming to ignore my less than pleasant demeanor at the moment. "How about we meet in the bar around six and I'll buy you a drink?"

I knew of girls who had things like that happen to them all the time. Girls who were constantly being hit on or who always had a group of guys around hanging onto every word they said. For the record, I was not one of those girls. Never had been. Never planned to be.

Which meant instead of being gracious or thrilled that he asked, I immediately thought he was up to something.

"Why?" I asked. "Do you normally invite newly arrived international women to meet you for drinks? Are you the resort welcoming committee? I wasn't told to expect you."

"No," he answered with an amused smile. "You'd be the first. And no I'm not on a committee."

I raised an eyebrow at him. The thing I'd learned early about overly handsome men is they almost always knew exactly how good looking they were, and they had a tendency to use that knowledge to their advantage.

"You don't believe me?" he asked.

"Not really."

He took that in stride. "I'm not really sure why I asked, to be honest, other than I saw you standing here, looking as if you're determined to have a nice time in Italy whether or not it kills you. And then as I'm trying to figure out why you would think it would be possible to not have a good time in Italy, you knocked your bag down." He shrugged. "You know the rest."

"Yes." I nodded, not even thinking about what I was getting ready to say. "You picked up my tampons."

"Is that what that was?" he asked, and it shocked me he didn't appear embarrassed or uneasy with the topic of conversation. "I was certain they were cotton swabs." He caught my what the heck look, and added, "I have a older sister."

"And if she was checking into a foreign hotel and a guy came up to her, asking if she'd like to meet up for a drink later, what would you tell her to do?" I couldn't say why I continued to stand there talking to him instead of heading up to find my room. Maybe it was the way his eyes seemed to dance with amusement, or the simple charm of his smile. I wasn't sure what it was, but something about him called to me in a way no one else ever had.

"If the guy was a known player," he said in reply to my question. "Then I'd have a problem with it. But, if he was sincere? That would be a different story altogether."

"True," I said. "The problem, though, is trying to determine how sincere he is."

"That's not a problem," he said, and I raised an eyebrow at him. He laughed and asked, "You don't believe me?"

"I don't see how it's not a problem."

"If you want to find out how sincere he is, you agree to meet him for the drink."

"Is that right?" I asked with a smile.

"Yes. It's truly the only way."

"There's only one more thing," I said and waited.

"And?"

"I don't know your name."

His grin returned. "Luca," he said, holding out his hand.

I take it in mine and do my best to ignore the electric spark I know I didn't imagine when our hands met. "Wren."

CHAPTER 5

LUCA

It wasn't until I heard her gasp, saw her eyes roll to the back of her head and her knees buckle that I realized it was her.

Wren.

"Wren!" I shouted, darting for her.

Fortunately, I was close enough that I could reach and catch her before she fell and cracked her head open. Cradling her in my arms, I carefully lifted her and walked to a nearby bench. I sat down, and within seconds, a security guard was at my side.

"Everything okay, sir?" he asked, eyeing the woman in my arms.

"Yes," I told him. "I'm sure she'll be fine. Just had a bit of a shock, is all. Perhaps if you could get a bottle of water?"

"Yes, of course," he said and took off.

A crowd of people had stopped what they'd been doing and ended their conversations when Wren collapsed. Now that nothing drastic seemed to be happening, no alien bursting out of her chest, no copious amount of blood involved, they quickly lost interest in the two of us, and went back to whatever they'd been doing before.

"Sir?"

I looked up to find a woman, a hotel employee, judging by the metal name tag she wore, holding a bottle of water and a damp cloth. The security guard I'd spoken with before stood in front of us, shielding us from curious eyes.

"Thank you," I said, taking the offered cloth and pressing it gently to Wren's forehead. At my touch, she stirred slightly, but didn't open her eyes.

The hotel employee placed the water beside me and within easy reach. "Do we need to call for medical help?"

I almost said no, but then realized I knew nothing of Wren's current medical condition or if she had anything in significant in her medical history. "I don't think so," I told her. "But I'm not one hundred percent certain. Let's give her a few minutes and we'll see how she's doing."

"Okay," she said. "My name is Marsha, and I'm the front manager on duty tonight. Let me know if you need anything, and if you don't see me, just ask anyone working and they'll be able to find me."

"Thank you, Marsha," I said, watching as she walked to the security guard and spoke to him.

Wren shifted in my arms and I turned my attention back to her. She hadn't opened her eyes yet, but I could see them moving underneath her eyelids. I took that as a positive sign. Hopefully, she'd wake up in the next few seconds.

"Wren," I whispered. "Open your eyes. It's okay. You're fine. Just a bit of a shock is all."

A bit? Ha! That was the understatement of the year. Possibly the entire decade. It seemed so surreal to be sitting on a bench in a hotel in Boston, holding in my arms the very woman I hadn't been able to get out of my mind for the last five years.

Her eyelids fluttered at the sound of her name. My fingers ached to touch her. Holding a damp cloth to her forehead wasn't enough. I wanted to brush my knuckles across her cheekbones, to trace the line of her jaw, and to discover if her skin was as soft as I remembered. I pushed the temptation away.

Then her eyes opened, and everything around us dissolved. The low level hum of activity from the people around us serving as background noise faded into nothing. For the briefest second, the entire universe consisted of two beings, me and her.

"Luca?" she asked.

"Yes."

She moved to sit up, and I begrudgingly let go. I picked up the water bottle and opened it before handing it to her.

"Thanks." She took one sip and then another, all the while looking at me as if I had two horns coming out of my head.

"What?" I finally asked. Surely I had nothing on my face.

"I keep expecting you to disappear into the thin air." She shook her head. "But you're still here."

Her answer wasn't what I expected, and I chuckled despite myself. "I could say the same thing about you."

"Why? How?" She shook her head and brought her hand up to touch her forehead. "This can't be real," she muttered to herself. Tentatively, she reached out and touched the flower in my lapel. "But it is, isn't it?"

"Yes," I whispered.

"You must be here to meet someone else."

"Why is that?" I didn't think Bachelor International would arrange for two couples to meet initially at the same time and place, but maybe they would. What did I know?

"Because I'm supposed to be meeting someone named Lucrezio. I've been told he's a boring recluse, and that in no way sounds like you."

Who the hell thought I was boring? "Lucrezio is my full name, but everyone calls me Luca. I'll own up to being somewhat reclusive, but I have to draw the line at boring."

She didn't respond to the boring comment, not that expected she would. "When did you find out you were meeting me?"

"The second I laid eyes on you."

Her confused expression made little sense until I realized much of the information on her would have been in the email Mia sent, still lounging around my inbox, unread. I reached into my pocket and pulled out my phone. "Mia sent me an email with information about you." I scrolled through my emails until I found the one I was searching for and opened it to read.

Wren Prescott

I'd had this email in my possession for how long? I was a damned idiot.

"Your last name is Prescott?" I asked.

"You didn't read your email?" she asked instead of answering, and I realized it wasn't the right time to tell her she was the reason I didn't open the email.

"It didn't seem necessary to read the email," I answer. "The date was set, you'd already been given the details. What good would come from reading the email?"

"You would at least know my last name."

"You're right," I said, not wanting to start an argument. "That reason along with many others."

She was silent for a long moment. "If you'd known it was me, would you have still shown up or would you have called Tenor and canceled?"

There were so many ways I could answer that question. What would she have done if she'd known it was me? Although I wasn't sure I wanted to know the answer to that one, I had a good idea I already knew how she'd reply.

Did I tell her I'd have said yes, because I wanted to see her? Had I not made that point very clear when she was in the hospital, refusing to see me? Or did I go the opposite reaction and answer no, I would abide by what she'd asked me for years ago, to walk away and let her go?

I could ignore her question and try to change the subject to something else.

I ended up telling her the truth. "If I'd read the email, and learned you were my match, I'd have called either Tenor or Mia and explained that you and I had met once before. That I was still wanting to have the date with you, but that they needed to get your approval first."

"That's what you would have done?" It looked like her eyes were a bit teary, but surely that was only my imagination. Why would Wren cry over a man she kicked out of her life years ago?

"Yes," I said, desperately wanting to know what answer she'd have given Tenor or Mia in that situation, but again being too damn scared to ask for fear of my little bird flying away once again.

It had been hard enough when she left me five years ago.

CHAPTER 6

LUCA

Five years ago

"What do you mean she's not a patient anymore?" I half yelled at the woman behind the desk. I knew, of course, she was just the messenger. She wasn't the one who'd released Wren from the hospital. Unfortunately for her, though, she was the only person I could talk to at the minute. "I was just here two hours ago and there was nothing said about her being released today."

I'd been nearly living at the hospital for the past several days. Spending most of my time in the tiny waiting area because Wren refused to see me. She'd actually refused all visitors, so it wasn't as if she'd singled me out. I couldn't stand the thought of her being in a hospital room alone. By herself, in a strange country, with people speaking a language she knew very little of.

And no one was talking about what happened or what sort of injuries she had.

Ski accident was all I heard. Ski accident. That was it. And that told me nothing.

The woman at the desk refused to get into an argument with me, which only made me more furious. Just as I was getting ready to launch another question at her, a door off to the side opened, and a tiny woman in a long white doctor's coat stepped out.

"Mr. Botticelli?" she asked.

"Yes," I replied, the fact that she knew my name momentarily cooling my rage.

"Come with me, please." She spoke in a commanding tone I'd not pictured someone of her stature having and turned without waiting or looking to see if I'd follow.

I hurried to catch up with her, needing to get to the door before it closed. She continued down the hall then made a right turn before stopping at the door of a small office.

Once we were both inside, she moved behind a desk to sit and pointed to a chair in front. "Have a seat."

I sat gingerly, leery about why I'd been brought back into this office.

"I am Dr. Ricci, and I was the primary doctor for Wren."

I nodded.

"Just so you are aware, anything I tell you, she gave me permission to pass along to you. Understand?"

I nodded again.

"Wren was discharged today because we have done all we can for her, medically, and she wanted to return home to the US as soon as possible."

I glanced at my watch, wondering if I left the hospital now, if I could make it to the airport and catch up with her before she took off.

"In case you're thinking about doing anything foolish," she said. "You should know that her plane has already taken off. My specific instructions were not to tell you anything until I was notified that she had left the country."

I narrowed my eyes, not quite believing her. "I wasn't aware international travel could be arranged so quickly."

"As I'm sure you know, the resort where the accident occurred has a certain reputation it would like to uphold. It was in their best interest to ensure this matter was dealt with as quickly and as quietly as possible."

I disliked this office and this doctor more and more with every passing second. "What you're saying is the resort wanted to get Wren out of the country as quickly as possible so she couldn't raise a stink?"

"I'm merely saying both sides got what they wanted, Mr. Botticelli."

"What is it Wren wanted you to tell me?"

"That she knows you've been staying here at the hospital, and that her wishes about seeing you have not changed. She requests that you not try to find or contact her." She took a deep breath. "I suggest you abide by her wishes. Wren has a tough road ahead of her. I'm afraid because of the amount of physical therapy she'll need, it's going to be a very long and painful road."

"Physical therapy?" I asked. "What kind and for how long? She's a dancer. That's what she loves."

"I'm afraid I've given you all the information I'm allowed, Mr. Botticelli."

"But you didn't give me anything!"

She leveled her gaze at me. "Are you going to make me call security?"

It was useless to attempt to get anything else out of her. The hardened lines of her face told me she wasn't bluffing about calling security, either. "No," I said to her. "I'm leaving."

I TRIED everything I could think of to track Wren down. Every resource I had, I used. Every favor I could collect on, I called in. I worked day and night to find her.

Months later, the only thing I had to show for my efforts was a long line of dead ends.

"She doesn't want to be found," Carmella told me, one day about three months after Wren had left. I'd just received a report back from the last investigator I had actively searching. As much as I wanted to think differently, I knew Carmella was right.

The time had come to cut my losses and accept the fact that Wren didn't want to be found. The truth was crushing, and part of me hated myself for allowing anyone to have such an impact on my life.

"Why don't you come to mama's for dinner tonight?" Carmella asked. "She's always asking after you, and she'd be delighted to see you and so would Gianna."

I swallowed my snort. I was certain Carmella's mama would be more than delighted to see me. She'd probably dance in the streets. She'd been trying to subtly and not so subtly push me together with Carmella since we were five. Carmella, on the other hand, wanted me for her best friend, Gianna, who spent so much time at Carmella's house, they could be sisters.

"I couldn't do that," I said. "I'd hate to impose on her."

"Please." Carmella rolled her eyes. "You know how much she cooks. There's no way you could be an imposition."

While we were both correct, I didn't want to be an imposition, and her mother always made enough to feed a small country. My actual concern was something completely different. If I showed up at her house for dinner, the news would be all over the grapevine within minutes. Someone would alert my sister, Maria, and in less than an hour, she'd be planning my wedding.

On the other hand, Gianna would be there. Though we had dated off-and-on throughout the years, she scoffed along with me whenever anyone tossed a hint our way about marriage.

Maybe Gianna was exactly what I needed at the moment. Someone to distract me from life for a few hours. I hadn't talked with her much since Wren left, but like Carmella said, my little bird had no plans to return. Even if she did, how would she be able to find me?

"Gianna will be there?" I asked.

Carmella nodded.

"I think I will," I told her. After all, what could it hurt?

I learned that night never to ask that question again.

CHAPTER 7

WREN

I was sure somewhere there was an etiquette guide on how to make small talk with a man you thought was The One, but in the end turned out not to be. Surely there was. Someone had to have written it, if for no other reason than to help their own self.

But if they had, I'd never found it. All I knew was that I was sitting almost entirely in Luca's lap. Not that he seemed to have a problem with my current position, but I thought it'd be best to leave no doubt in his mind that nothing of the sort was on my mind.

Well, it was, but I wouldn't admit that to him.

I placed the half empty water bottle down on the floor at our feet and shifted my body so it wasn't touching his any more. Luca frowned and I seriously considered scooting back closer to him. Not because of his frown, but because of how cold the parts of me that had been touching him became.

I told myself to deal with it. I'd lived the last five years without the warmth of Luca's touch, I wasn't going to shatter into a million pieces at its absence now. At least I hoped I didn't. Luca lifted his hand, and for a split second, I thought he would touch me. My breath caught in my throat because I wanted it so badly. I allowed memories I'd forbidden myself to remember flood my mind. My eyes closed as I recalled the way his fingers had once swept across my skin. His insistence on not leaving one inch of my body untouched had awoken me like no one else.

Aware I'd probably start moaning if I didn't think about something else, I opened my eyes. Luca sat at my side, leaning forward with his fingers entwined. Waiting?

For me?

I cleared my throat to get his attention. "I'm feeling much better if you want to head to the reception now."

He glanced at his watch. "The reception ended about ten minutes ago, and I'm sure they've started dinner service."

"Do you want to try to make the dinner?"

"No, I don't want to arrive late."

I winced. "I'm sorry. I totally screwed up your night."

"You did no such thing," he said.

I wasn't sure how he possibly came to that conclusion. Not logically, anyway. Of course I'd screwed up his night. At that very moment, he was supposed to be having dinner, and instead, he was sitting in the lobby with me because I'd passed flat out when I recognized him. I opened my mouth to tell him that very thing, but he stopped me.

"I didn't want to go that stuffy reception and dinner to begin with, so I should thank you for giving me an excuse not to attend. And trust me, if I really wanted to be there, I would go."

I nodded. That made sense. "What do we do now?" I asked. The shock of seeing him again had faded somewhat and it was sinking in that Luca was here, in Boston, sitting beside me. My mind had tricked itself over the years that Luca was nothing, and meant nothing, but my heart had done no such thing, and not only was it aware of how close he was, but it was alerting my body to that very fact.

He turned to face me more fully, and I knew immediately he felt the same. "I don't know," he said. "All I know is I don't want our evening to end right now."

I dipped my head briefly. "Me either, but I don't want to talk about the past tonight." I looked up to see if he understood and felt the same.

I couldn't tell if he understood or not. All his expression conveyed to me was he was fighting a war inside. What was he battling? Had I read him wrong?

"But, you know," I said to give him an out. "If you don't want to do anything, it's okay. I understand. I mean—"

He interrupted by taking my face in hands and pressing his lips to mine in a kiss that spoke of his own longings over the years we'd been apart. I let myself get lost in his kiss and shut the door in my mind to keep anything other than the moment and Luca outside.

The broken part of me tried to give a warning. Tried telling me I'd already walked down this road once and that the second journey would not end any differently. I slammed the door in its face. I'd already been about as broken as a person could be. If tonight was all Luca and I had, I planned to grab onto it with both hands and hold on for as long as possible.

He broke the kiss, but kept his hands on me, as if he feared I'd run if given the chance, and when he spoke, his voice was labored. "Come to my room. We can order room service."

I remembered the days and nights we'd spent in his room in Italy. We'd stayed locked away from the real world, either wrapped up with each other in bed, or just lounging around, talking. Every so often we'd leave so he could show me around his country, or we'd find a quiet and out of the place to eat when we grew tired of room service. It had been the best period of time in my life, and now, for one night at least, I could have those days back.

There really was no decision to make.

"No talking?" I asked, just to be certain.

He pulled back enough to look into my eyes. "We won't do anything you don't want to."

He'd broken my heart in Italy. It'd probably be shattered again when he left, but at the moment I didn't care. I'd lived five years without him, but not a day went by that I didn't think about him, didn't long for him, and that I didn't regret the way I'd left things.

This wouldn't be a do-over because those were impossible. What it would be was a do again. A better option in my mind, anyway.

He still held my face in his hands, but his forehead was wrinkled. Did he think I was going to say no? I nearly laughed. There was no probability of that happening. "Lead the way."

His eyes widened in surprise. He had thought I was going to turn him down. "Are you sure?" he asked.

I felt emboldened by his uncertainty. I slipped my hands from where they rested around his shoulders, down his back, until they rested just above his ass. His eyes grew dark with need, causing mine to do the same. All said, we probably weren't being entirely appropriate for being in public, but at the moment I didn't care.

I kept my hands where they were, holding him in place, and I shifted my hips, pressing myself against him. He sucked in a breath as I moved against his erection. My own caught in my throat at the same time. I'd forgotten how large he was.

"Be sure, Wren."

"I've never ached for anyone the way I ache for you," I told him. "In fact, the only thing I'm sure about at this moment is how much I want you to take me to your room."

CHAPTER 8

LUCA

I no longer felt as if I resided in the real world. It seemed more likely I'd somehow stepped through a portal or a wormhole or something similar and ended up in an alternate universe. There was no other way to explain how Wren was in my arms. I'd never before felt like I needed to ask someone to pinch me to ensure I wasn't sleeping.

But even in my dreams, Wren had never appeared to me so open, so soft, so needy. I wanted to kiss her again, but she'd asked for me to take her to my room, and I told myself I could wait until we were no longer in public to have my lips on her again.

Though I'd already asked and she'd confirmed that yes, she was certain my room was where she wanted to go; I hesitated. Only for a half second, but it was a half second she picked up on.

"Unless you don't want to?" she asked.

Idiot, I scolded myself. Now she thought I didn't want her, when in fact, that couldn't be further from the truth. I wanted her too much. So much that I'd trade anything to have another chance with her.

"There's nothing I want more," I assured her.

To prove it, I slipped my hand into hers. She gave me a little smile, and we made our way across the lobby to the elevator bank. While we waited, I couldn't stop myself from stroking my thumb across her knuckles. Her skin felt softer, and I couldn't help but wonder what other differences there were between the Wren I knew then and the woman currently at my side.

Though I'd vowed to myself I would wait until we were alone and locked behind the privacy of my suite's doors before I placed my lips on her again, I made no such promise about the other parts of my body. My hands had to be on her somewhere. It didn't matter how. I'd be just as happy holding her hand as I'd be with my arm wrapped around her shoulders or waist. As long as we were touching in some way, I'd survive not having my lips on her just yet. At least for a minute or two.

She'd made it very clear that talking was out of the question. I had no problem going along with her request, however, I wanted to tease her about it. Several people got into the elevator with us, and since we'd be the last to get off, I pulled her into a back corner.

Once the doors closed, I lowered my head to her ear and whispered, "I'm going to need a bit of clarification on the no talking rule. Do you mean no talking about certain subjects or no talking period?"

She tried to look around me. I supposed to see if anyone overhead, but I blocked her way.

"Is dirty talking allowed?" I asked and nibbled on her ear. "Am I allowed to say that even though you look sexy as hell in that dress, I can't wait to get it off of you?"

"Luca," she half moaned in warning, but I wasn't about to stop.

"Is asking you a question off limits? Or can I ask how you want to take my cock the first time?"

I took a step closer to her, meaning to ask her something else when she pulled my head down and whispered, "To answer your third question, yes, it's allowed, and to answer your fifth, I want it so hard and so deep, there's no way I'll look back and think this is all a dream tomorrow."

It took all I had not to push her against the wall, hike her gown up to her waist, and take her there in the elevator. "I believe that can be arranged."

By that time, we were the only ones left on the elevator. I stepped back, wanting to put space between us for at least the next little bit. We'd waited this long, surely we could wait the handful of minutes it would take to get into my room. The doors of the elevator opened silently, and we stepped into the cool air of the hallway.

There were only six guest rooms on the floor, and I placed my hand low on Wren's back to steer her to the correct door. Within seconds, we were inside, picking up where we had left off. Her hands slid down my back as I worked to unzip her gown.

Even though we were both adults, and we were doing something we'd both agreed to, I couldn't help but think we should talk. Wren had been the one to suggest otherwise, and I hadn't verbalized any objections, but it didn't sit right with me. We'd had ten crazy, passionate days together, and I'd fallen harder and faster than I'd ever thought possible. Yet, she'd been able to move on as if it had been nothing to her.

I wanted to sit her down and ask why? Why had she left me so suddenly? Why had she not allowed me to see her in the hospital? Why had it been five years since I last saw her, and that it was only by coincidence I saw her now?

But for the moment, my questions would have to go unanswered, because no talking had been her only request, and I'd have agreed to a lot more than that for the opportunity to have her in my arms again.

I gave up trying to unzip her. With as much experience as I had with clothes, you'd think I'd be better able to work a zipper. She was fumbling with the buttons on my shirt, so I shrugged out of my jacket to make it easier for her to get the thing off of me. Once the shirt joined my jacket on the floor, she reached for my waist, but I shook my head. It was her turn.

"Turn around," I said.

She did so slowly, and for a moment, I stood where I was and took in the sight of her, still unable to fully comprehend she was here. Her head turned slightly as if she looked to find me. I lifted her hair and placed a kiss on her nape.

"Am I taking too long?" I asked.

"Just wondering if there's a problem."

"The only problem is I don't know what to do with you first."

"You could help me get this gown off," she suggested. "I'm pretty sure that'd be a step in the right direction."

"Still sarcastic, I see."

"I need to know this is real."

She wanted real? I'd give her real. And I'd make it so real, and so good, she'd never question herself again. I didn't speak those words to her, though. Words meant nothing without action behind them.

Moving without making a noise, I eased the zipper down her back, inch by inch, revealing the skin underneath the gown's silken material. When I reached her lower back, I slid first one sleeve and then the other off her shoulders, letting the gown fall to a puddle at her feet. She stepped away from it, but didn't turn to face me. The gown obviously hadn't allowed for a bra, as she only had on a tiny pair of panties. She wasn't embarrassed, was she?

It was possible she was. Five years could change a lot on a person's body. Though from what I saw, Wren had nothing to be embarrassed about. How well I remembered her strong legs wrapped around my waist. My amazement at the muscles I'd found the first time I stroked her upper thigh.

They looked toned, but nowhere near as muscular as they'd been. Wasn't that odd? It'd been five years, shouldn't they be the same, if not more muscular?

An odd mark on the inside of her knee caught my eye. A scar?

"Luca?" Wren asked, turning around.

I didn't look at her face, but instead kept my attention focused on her legs. At the sight of the healed, but obscenely long scars on the front of them both, all the breath left my body. I gulped in air and managed to get out, "What happened to your legs?"

"We said no talking." Her voice was cold and hard. With one glance, I saw her expression matched.

She was correct, but I wanted to argue that this was different. I'd assumed she'd meant no talking about their past in Italy, and this had nothing to do about our time there.

My gaze dropped from her eyes to her legs and then back again. Or did it? "What aren't you telling me?"

"Why do you keep asking me questions? My requirement, my only requirement was no talking."

"Did this happen in Italy?" I asked.

She didn't have to say anything, I saw my answer in her expression. Completely stunned, I couldn't speak for a long second. "Wren, I'm so—"

"No!" She interrupted, holding her hand out as if wanting to catch or stop my words before they made it out into the universe.

I stopped and watched helplessly as she stepped into her dress.

"Don't go," I said, even as she zipped herself up, gathered her purse, and walked to the door. "Please."

She spun around, her eyes wet, but not from sad tears. Oh no, not those. Wren was mad as hell, and those were angry-as-fuck tears.

"Don't please me," she said. "I told you I didn't want to talk. You agreed. Then we get up here and you repeatedly try to get me to answer questions about things I obviously didn't want to I discuss."

I had no argument for her because there was truth in every word she spoke. She'd wanted one night. There hadn't been a day that went by in the last five years, I hadn't thought of her at least once. Not one night passed that I wouldn't have traded anything to have one more night with her.

Then miracle of miracles, she walks back into my life, offers me exactly what I want with her only stipulation being that I kept my damn mouth closed. And somehow that was too hard for me to do. I was officially the dumbest asshole who ever lived.

"Let me at least call a cab for you," I said, but she shook her head.

"No need. Either there'll be one downstairs waiting, or concierge will call one for me."

She was determined to leave, and to do so on her terms and her terms only. And I had to accept that none of those terms involved me.

"There's no excuse for my behavior," I said. "Every word you spoke is true. I hope to see you again someday, but if not, I'll be forever grateful I had the opportunity to see you again."

She didn't turn around for the door the way I thought she would, but remained still and unmoving with such a pained expression it physically hurt me. I'd rarely felt so useless. I wanted to take her into my arms, whisper how sorry I was. I needed to tell her that I wasn't sure what I'd done, but that I'd move heaven and earth to make it right and to see her smile again. But I didn't reach for her, knowing my embrace would be rejected. And I wanted to spare myself the heartbreak of her rejection.

One lone tear ran down her cheek before she turned and left. As the door clicked closed behind her, I nearly pulled my hair out in anguish. Not reaching for her hadn't spared me anything. I still hurt like hell. Having experienced the pain of such intense heartbreak before, I knew of only one way to make it go away. I walked to the well-stocked bar I'd noticed earlier in the day.

Looked like it was going to be a drink for one kind of night.

CHAPTER 9

WREN

ONCE I MADE IT HOME, I sent Mia a text.

I'm home. Date was fine. Talk tomorrow.

I wrote it concise and vague, hoping she'd read between the lines, take the hint, and leave it at that. Thankfully, her reply was quick.

Fine doesn't sound good. Want to do lunch tomorrow? Meet at BI office and leave from there?

I sent back a message telling her that sounded great, and I'd see her then. I hadn't allowed myself to think about Luca, and I still wasn't ready. I purposely kept my mind blank and just went through the motions of getting undressed, slipping on my favorite pajamas, and cleaning my face. Finally, I made some hot tea and, curling up on the couch, thought back over the night.

That Luca would see the scars on my legs never crossed my mind until he brought them up. I felt like an idiot. And a pathetic one at that, because surely, if anyone had seen me naked in the past five years, I'd have been prepared. I let no one see my legs and the numerous scars on them. My year round wardrobe consisted of long pants and long skirts. Whenever I wore a shorter skirt, I always paired it with thick tights so the scars weren't visible.

And yet tonight, when my gown slipped to the floor, and even as I stepped out of it, not once did my brain clue in and think about my legs being on display. If I thought about it logically, there was no reason not to tell Luca what happened.

Illogically, there were several. To start with, I didn't want to see the pity in his eyes. And it would be there. How could it not be when he would undoubtedly remember how much dancing meant to me? Another reason was pride. During our time together, Luca had commented several times about how impressive he found the muscles in my legs. My legs were still strong, but nowhere near what they had been five years ago.

Did that make me petty? To be perfectly honest, I didn't care.

MIA WAS WAITING for me in the lobby of the building Bachelor International was located in when I arrived to meet her for lunch. She was alone. Though I hadn't expected Tenor to be joining us for lunch, it wouldn't have surprised me if he'd been standing with her.

"Where's your other half?" I teased. "Is he really letting you out of his sight for lunch? I thought he might be here to see you off or something."

"We are not that bad." Mia rolled her eyes. "And he's in a meeting."

"We'll have to agree to disagree on the not that bad part," I said. "Where do you want to go for lunch?"

She named a nearby deli we both liked and was within walking distance. I agreed, adding we could eat outside at one of the many tables they had for that purpose.

"Yes," Mia said. "Before you know it, it'll be too cold to eat outside."

"Ugh, don't remind me." It was no secret I loved everything about Boston, except for the winters.

"Every winter you swear you're going to move to Florida and you never do," she said as we neared the deli. "I think you secretly love the winter, and you only bring up Florida so people think you don't like the winter."

"I have no reason to make up something like that. One day I'll call you up from my seaside condo, and you'll be so jealous."

"If you move to Florida and don't tell me about it until you're settled into your seaside condo, you won't have to worry about me being jealous. I'll be mad as hell and won't talk to you ever again."

I nodded, knowing I would never do such a thing. "Completely understood."

We'd reached the deli and placed our orders inside and then walked to the outside to claim a table while we waited for our food.

I was impressed with Mia's patience. She waited until they brought our sandwiches to the table before saying, "Tell me how last night went."

"You know the guy from Italy I told you about?" I'd only recently told Mia about my time in Italy, and how I'd met a guy there.

She placed her sandwich on her plate. "The one you wouldn't let visit you in the hospital? The one who's the reason you've dated no one since Italy?"

"Yes," I said. "Him."

"What about him?"

"He was my date last night. Your client."

Mia had a potato chip in her hand, and it was midway to her mouth, but it stilled at my words. "No way."

"Yes way."

"Holy shit, Wren." Her eyes were wide with shock. "What did you do?"

I snorted, which made her look even more shocked. "The first thing I did was faint. Fortunately, he had quick reflexes, and could catch me before I face-planted and broke my nose or worse."

"You fainted?" Mia asked. "Are you okay now?"

"Yes," I assured her. "Not even a headache."

"I've never heard of you fainting before."

"I don't think I ever had before last night."

Mia lifted an eyebrow. "Either way, you don't think you should go get checked out by a doctor just to make sure you're okay?"

"Nah. It was a reaction to seeing him again after all this time. Either that or because I couldn't believe the man Tenor thought was so boring was also the man I knew from Italy."

"Oh my god," Mia said, excitement filling her expression and voice. "Do you have any idea what this means?"

I looked at her warily. "Not really, and to be honest, based on how excited you look at the moment, I'm not sure I want to know. It has nothing to do with me going on another date, does it?"

"No, the exact opposite, in fact."

Her words made little sense, but as long as she wasn't going to guilt me into another date, I was okay being patient until she explained. Which, based on how excited she looked, would be sooner, rather than later.

She leaned forward, as if she had a secret she was dying to tell. "You and Lucrezio were the first couple matched with the new system I put into place. Remember how I said your match had the highest numbers?"

I nodded.

"I predicted the two of you would be a good match," she said. "And I was right." She sat back in her seat. "Now, tell me what happened after you fainted at the sight of him, and he caught you in his arms."

Based on her dreamy tone of voice, she probably thought the worst thing that happened yesterday was that I fainted. I wasn't sure how detailed I wanted to be.

"We talked for a little while," I said. "And when we finally got around to looking at the time, we realized the reception would be over, and Luca didn't want to show up for dinner late."

I paused. Across the table, Mia waited. I decided to give her an abbreviated version.

"Neither one of us felt like going out, so we ended up in his room. We planned to order room service." Mia's eyes grew wide with surprise. She probably assumed we actually did what Luca and I had intended to do when I agreed to go to his room. "But when we made it to his room, he kept wanting to talk about the past. I repeatedly told him I didn't want to discuss it, but he kept bringing it up. I eventually gave up, left his room, and went home."

It took her a minute to speak. "That was not the way I envisioned your night going when you said you agreed to go to his room."

"That makes three of us."

She somehow looked as down as I felt about the entire thing. Part of me couldn't help but wonder if it was because she just lost the ability to use me as a success story in her newest marketing campaign. I knew it was callous for me to think that of her, but the alternative, that I was wearing my heart on my sleeve, was too much to take in. I'd worked hard to disguise my emotions. Surely I hadn't lost the ability to do so after my unexpected reunion with Luca.

"So," Mia said. "What are you going to do next?"

Her question caught me off-guard. It still seemed surreal that after five years my path had once more crossed Luca's. I didn't have an answer for her, but it did bring up a new revelation. Now that our lives had intersected again, I needed a plan, or at least something that halfway resembled one for how to handle Luca. I had a sinking feeling in my gut that pretending he didn't exist wouldn't work.

CHAPTER 10

WREN

AFTER THE ACCIDENT IN ITALY, and the eventual acceptance of the fact that I would never dance professionally, I realized I had to come up with some way to support myself.

I never gave much thought as to what I'd do with my life if I didn't dance. When you're young, the thought that something could come along and leave both you and your life unrecognizable is unfathomable. Your mind can process that it happens in some vague way to other people, but not to you.

And when it does happen to you, you feel as if you've been tricked. Like all your life you've accepted XYZ, and then someone shows up and tells you it's not XYZ, it never was XYZ, and it never will be XYZ. But don't despair, you can have some lovely ABC. You soon learn that while you can get by with ABC, it'll never be XYZ.

If ballet was my XYZ, journalism was my ABC.

Journalism had never been a burning passion of mine, and I didn't see it ever becoming one. In my mind, it would always be that thing I had to do when I could no longer dance. The only positive thing being, I was pretty good at what I did. As one would expect, I decided early to keep my ambivalence about my job to myself.

Almost two hours after my lunch with Mia, I was fairly certain the look I gave my supervising editor, Zach, was the same look I'd have given him if he started speaking Latin to me. In fact, after hearing what he said, I really wished he had been speaking Latin because that would mean I'd have had no idea what I'd just heard.

Unfortunately for me, he'd spoken in plain English, and even with his heavy Bostonian accent, I could still understand my latest assignment, an in-depth look at the gentleman making news in the Italian fashion industry, and the relocation of his business to the US.

In other words, Luca.

"Is there a problem, Wren?" he asked. "I thought you'd be excited about the assignment, but you look like I've kicked your dog."

I gave him a fake smile, but in my mind, I couldn't help but think that if I hadn't been as good at the job I merely put up with, if I'd sucked just a bit, I wouldn't be the staffer "rewarded" with the assignment.

Zach didn't seem to know what to do with my lack of excitement. "It'll be an easy piece to write. Fluff. Think human interest story. You know how much our readers eat that shit up. And, you heard the part about the travel?"

Yes, I had, but I let him repeat it because it seemed as if he enjoyed doing so.

"First class all the way," he said. "From flights, to accommodations, to food. You'll basically be living the high life on someone else's dime."

He said that last sentence as if it's everyone's dream to mooch off of those who are better off than themselves.

News flash, Zach.

It's not.

I held my hand up to get him to stop. Which, mercifully, he did. "I'll do it. I'll write the story, but why do I have to travel with him?"

It was bad enough I'd been selected to write the story in the first place, but the second part of the assignment was for me to travel to Italy when he left and to stay there with him until he returned to the States some time in the following week.

"Because when you're with him, you'll see what really makes him tick," Zach said. "You'll get a better insight on him this way than you would with a mere interview."

"I can tell you now what makes him tick," I said. "First and foremost, he's a player. He likes easy women."

"A player?" Zach asked, his tone insinuating my statement was almost the craziest thing he'd ever heard. "Are you sure we're talking about the same guy?"

"I can't imagine there are two men named Lucrezio Botticelli who happen to be famous fashion designers."

"I'm sure you're right, which means I'm not certain who or where you got your information, but it's wrong."

Zach spoke with a confidence that nearly made me question myself. Especially when I paired it with the knowledge that he was rarely wrong about these things. But the truth of it was, in this case, I was the one who was right. After all, I was speaking from experience.

If I needed proof, all I had to do was recall the short amount of time it took for him to invite me to his room the night before. Not that I minded in fact just the opposite. I wanted to go to his room, and had never been happier that he was a player, because I knew he'd make my time worthwhile. Had he not pissed me off by refusing to shut the hell up the multiple times I'd asked, I know the night would have been spectacular.

If I told Zach that I knew Luca personally, there was a possibility he'd remove me from the assignment. But it was hard to know with any certainty how he'd react or what he'd do. He could just as easily say my relationship would offer additional insights. Probably for the best to keep that information in my back pocket for the time being.

As I was thinking of the best way to reply, an idea came to mind. If I took this assignment, and from the looks of it, I really had little choice about the whole thing, I could paint Luca in any light I wanted. He might have lulled people into believing he was something he wasn't, but I could make those same people believe anything I wanted them to about him.

"I guess I'll be able to find out for certain, won't I?" I said in response to his earlier statement about my information being wrong. I didn't follow up that I didn't get my information on Luca being a player from any person or any other type of source, but that it was based on personal experience. Hell, I'd only recently told Mia about him, I wasn't about to go yelling it to the entire world. Nor was I about to tell him or anyone else who didn't already know that I'd had a date with him the night before.

"Does that mean you're going to take the assignment?" he asked.

"Do I have a choice?" I replied instead of giving a yes or no answer.

Zach frowned. "You always have a choice, Wren. I might be disappointed if you didn't want to do it, because I think you're the best writer I have for this story, but I'd reassign it to someone else if you were opposed for a particular reason."

I translated that to mean I didn't have to accept, but that if I didn't, he'd more than likely give me crap assignments for the next year.

"So when does this whole deal start?" I asked.

Zach picked up a few sheets of paper from his desk, stacked them together in a pile, and handed them to me. "Here's what the travel agency pulled together for you. It's an itinerary, subject to change, of course, and the information we sent to Mr. Botticelli's personal assistant, so she'd know what our plans were for the article and the travel situation. It doesn't have your information listed yet because I wanted to talk to you before sending anything over to their office. Also, now that I've talked with you, and you've agreed to take the assignment, I'll have the agency get the travel arrangements made."

He paused for a second. Was he expecting me to read all the information right then and there? I glanced at the pile of papers because he still hadn't answered my question. There were no dates whatsoever listed, at least on the top page. Thinking back to the night before and the time I'd spent with Luca, had he mentioned anything about when he'd be leaving Boston, and if he'd be going back to Italy when he left? I couldn't remember that he had.

"As for when the assignment starts," Zach said, finally getting around to what I'd asked in the first place. "Mr.

Botticelli is leaving Boston and the US in two days. You need to go with him, so I'm afraid that doesn't give you much time to pack or prepare. I hope that isn't a problem for you? I'm sorry I couldn't give you more time. Everything came down from upper management so quickly..."

He didn't have to say anything else, because with those few words, I knew exactly why I'd been the one chosen for the assignment. I was single, with no significant other, no steady date, no children, no commitments to anything outside of work. Zach had just got out of his mouth it was a last minute request from the men upstairs.

And what do you do with a last minute assignment that involves a lot of travel?

You give it to Wren. She has nothing better to do, anyway.

I decided, standing there in front of Zach. I'd do the piece on Luca, but it would be the last thing I wrote. Life was too short to spend it doing something you just fell into. I wasn't sure exactly what I wanted to do, but I knew I'd spent enough time mourning a dream that would never happen. It was time to move on.

CHAPTER 11

LUCA

I CHECKED MY WATCH AGAIN, wondering why I thought it'd been a good idea to agree to a local magazine's request for one of their writers to travel with me and cover my relocation to the States. Then I remembered. Oh right, the request had come through the morning after Wren left. I'd had a hangover from hell, thanks to the copious amount of alcohol I'd downed the night before in my unsuccessful attempt to numb the pain of Wren walking away from me.

Actually, the more I thought about it, I wasn't sure I'd agreed necessarily, but rather my reply had been, "Sure, why the hell not?"

Sober and no longer hungover, I was pissed at the situation. Not that I had anyone to blame other than myself. I was the one who drank too much and therefore brought on the hangover. It was me who insisted on answering my phone instead of allowing Carmella to handle everything. One positive thing about the flight back to Italy was that Carmella wouldn't be on board. I'd asked her to remain in Boston to work on the administrative tasks that needed completing.

I arrived at the private airstrip early. Though I was ready, no one else appeared to be. It didn't take long for me to determine that because my mood was so foul, I had no business being in anyone's company. I acknowledged as much and confined myself to the back of the plane where I could wait alone and hopefully no one would bother me. I didn't care about being polite or welcoming whatever poor sod got roped into covering me. From the way it sounded, we'd have plenty of bonding time during the next few days.

It wasn't normal for me to be in such a horrible disposition. I chalked it up to the bad way I'd handled my second chance with Wren, and how I'd pretty much ensured she'd never want to see me again. She hadn't merely walked out of my life this time, I'd all but shoved her out the door by not abiding by her wishes.

My plan to hide away in the back of the plane worked beautifully because other than one of the flight attendants, Brigitta, who stopped by only long enough to ensure I was ready for takeoff, no one came near me. I assumed word of my less than pleasant disposition had spread. Though I heard chatter from the front of the plane, I remained alone in my self imposed isolation.

I'd known the isolation wouldn't last long. Not since Brigitta was working. I'd traveled more in the past four months than I had in the four years prior. When you travel that frequently, you get to know people.

Brigitta worked for the company I contracted with for private flights. We'd often chat whenever time allowed during a flight. She was from England and as we spoke and got to know each other, I'd learned she had an impressive background. I'd asked her what it was about her current job she liked, because I couldn't see her working as a flight attendant for the span of her career.

She'd laughed and said each flight with client was an educational experience. I didn't push, but I had a feeling there was more below the surface she wasn't ready to reveal to anyone just yet.

As expected, Brigitta made her way back to my section of the plane about twenty minutes after we took off. She sat down in the captain's chair beside me with a smile and a nod.

"Word from the flight crew is you're in somewhat of a mood," she said.

"That certainly explains why you're back here," I replied, knowing I could get away with teasing her.

She rolled her eyes. "I thought you'd at least come and introduce yourself to your new charge, the journalist."

"If I am in *somewhat of a mood*," I said. "Then it's probably for the best that I don't meet them right this minute. I'm sure I'll feel more like myself after I decompress for a bit. I'll go introduce myself in an hour or so."

Brigitta stood up. "I'll let you rest then. Do you need anything?"

"If you could see to it that I'm not disturbed, I'd appreciate it."

She nodded and left.

I KEPT to myself in the back of the plane for most of the flight, and most of it, I'd spent asleep. I'd never functioned well traveling internationally, and this trip hadn't been any different. Unfortunately, my calendar for the week ahead promised little recuperation time. Nearly every day held multiple meetings requiring my attendance.

The most important thing I could do was to stay sober. An action I told myself wouldn't be hard to accomplish since Wren would be on the other side of the world. Though I'd been known to overindulge, albeit most of those times were years ago, the only times I'd ever been drunk off my ass were because of Wren.

I awoke and discovered there were another two hours before we landed. Feeling more rested and in a much better mood, I drank some water and freshened up in the bathroom. Then, deciding there was no better time than the present, and finding no reason to delay the inevitable, I made my way toward the front of the plane.

May, the woman helping in Carmella's absence, lounged on a love seat with papers scattered a table in front of her. For her sake, I hoped the plane didn't hit any pockets of turbulence or else it would not be a good day for her.

Two junior assistants, Richard and Wayne, sat on the love seat opposite May's. They both had laptops out and headphones on.

All three of them appeared to be busy, and I didn't want to interrupt. Besides, they weren't my focus for the moment. Brigitta stood nearby, ready to offer assistance if needed. She glanced up, her eyes questioning if I needed anything. I gave my head a quick shake. In front of the pair of love seats were two rows of captain's chairs, much like the ones in the back where I'd sequestered myself.

Only one seat was occupied. A woman, based on the long hair the color I'd heard described as dirty blond before. As one who spent much of his life dealing and working with color, I'd always thought of dirty blond as an absolutely horrid way to describe someone's hair. It made it sound unkempt and, well, *dirty*. Ash blond wasn't much of an improvement to my mind. Golden blond, honey blond, even bronzed or umber blonde sounded better.

Whatever color you wanted to call it, the woman with the brownish blond hair was asleep based on the way her head leaned to one side. I probably should have shoved my foul mood aside earlier when she boarded and introduced myself. Now I just felt like the ass I knew I was.

"She hasn't been out for very long," Brigitta said, as if that gave me permission to wake her up.

"That's okay," I said. "Let her rest. I'll sit up here." And try to think of an appropriate way to apologize, I added in my head.

I decided against taking a seat in the same section she was sitting in and instead sat across the aisle from where she slept. From the corner of my eye, I saw Brigitta turn to answer a question from May.

I tried to think about the week before me and everything I had to take care of, but my gaze kept returning to the sleeping woman across the aisle from me. The more I looked at the back of her head, the more it seemed familiar. But I didn't see how that was possible. It wasn't as if I spent a lot of time looking at the back of people's heads, after all.

Funny. I'd assumed the reporter sent to shadow me would be a male. I'm not sure why I made that assumption, but whenever I envisioned someone following me around for the next few days, it was always a man I pictured.

It was the color, I finally decided, after looking at the back of the reporter's hair. It was the same as Wren's. Satisfied there was nothing more than hair color striking me as familiar about the reporter, I settled in my seat, preparing to wait until the reporter woke up.

CHAPTER 12

WREN

THANK goodness Luca thought I was sleeping. I wasn't sure how much longer I'd be able to pretend I was napping, or even if I should continue the ruse. Maybe the best thing to do would be to confront Luca and demand he have the plane turn around and return to Boston. I didn't care how much Zach tried to pressure me into taking this assignment, I'd have never in a million years agreed to it if I'd known Carmella was in any way currently associated with Luca.

We'd just boarded the plane and while we waited for the final preparations to be made, I'd listlessly scrolled to the bottom of the email detailing my travel arrangements. That's when I spotted her name.

I knew Carmella from my last trip to Italy. She'd worked for him then and to say she didn't care for me was putting it mildly. Carmella had disliked me from the moment she spied me having a drink with Luca on the day I arrived. At the time, I couldn't understand her disdain, and assumed I'd done something wrong. But as Luca and I grew closer, and the days went on, I realized what her problem was. She wanted Luca for herself. I could have been anyone, and she'd have hated me.

I kept my head turned away from Luca as I went through my options. Unfortunately, getting the plane to turn around and return to Boston wasn't plausible. Neither was flying back once we made it to our location. Now that I'd had over ten seconds to think about the situation, I realized that just seeing her name at the bottom of an email didn't mean anything. Five years ago, she'd been his constant shadow whenever she could find him. Obviously, things had changed. At least the bitch wasn't on the plane.

And when I said "bitch" it was with massive apologies to all female dogs.

I wasn't sure if Luca knew who I was. Zach had never told me who his point person was, so while I knew someone on his team knew my name, I could only assume it wasn't him.

And since I'd mentioned his name in my head, it was probably time to pretend like I was waking up. Better to let Luca realize who would follow him around sooner, rather than later. And it was already late enough. I'd been peeved when I realized he was staying in the back of the plane by himself. Then I'd heard mumbles about his mood and how it was a bad one.

I'd never been around Luca when he'd been in a foul mood. But from what I could tell by listening to the staff members traveling with them, it wasn't a pleasant experience. When one guy noticed me eavesdropping, he was quick to add that it was a good thing it didn't happen all that often.

I gave a half yawn and stretched a bit, not sure my performance was all that believable, but it was the best I could come up with on short notice. Acting was never one of my strengths. Most of the time, whatever I thought was plastered all over my face.

I shifted my seat back from being reclined to a more upright position. Only then did I very slowly look around the cabin, leaving the side where I assumed Luca sat for last. Whether I'd be met with resigned acceptance or complete disbelief, I wasn't sure.

As he came into view, his jaw dropped and he looked like he'd seen a ghost. Complete disbelief it was. Honestly, if I'd wagered a bet of which of the two reactions it'd have been, resigned acceptance would have won my vote. I'd assumed he'd been made aware of who I was, and I caused his foul mood. That just goes to show you how consumed we all are about ourselves and how we assume everything has to do with us. Like I was the only thing in the world able to make Luca be in a foul mood. Surely that honor could be claimed by many people.

I lifted my lips in a slight grin. From all appearances, he was still trying to wrap his head around the fact I'd been the one assigned to him.

"Hello, Luca," I said, because it became clear very quickly he wouldn't talk first. "Small world, isn't it?"

He didn't answer my question, instead he replied, "I thought they'd assign a guy to me."

Not missing a beat, I quipped back, "Unfortunately, you're stuck with me. Is that going to be an issue for you? Because I doubt we'd be able to make it back to Boston on the gas that's left in the plane."

"No," he said, but I got the idea he was trying to convince himself more than he was replying to me. "I didn't know you were a reporter. That wasn't what I thought you'd be doing."

"It's not exactly what I thought I'd be doing, either. So I guess that makes two of us."

I was pretty certain there'd be no need for me to explain why I was a reporter rather than the dancer I was sure he thought I'd be. He had seen the scars on my legs and probably knew with only one glance they were nowhere near as strong or muscular as they'd been five years ago.

"How long have you been a reporter?" he asked.

It was the exact question I'd wanted to avoid when I'd been in his hotel room not too long ago. Unlike that night, however, I had nowhere to go while stuck on a plane.

I matched his stare and refused to waver. "Going on five years."

"You're not a dancer?"

If there was a question I hated more, I wasn't sure what it could be. Wasn't it obvious I wasn't a dancer? Part of me wanted to claim that of course I was a dancer. Once a dancer, always a dancer, and all that jazz. But the bigger part of me accepted that in order to be considered a dancer, one had to dance.

"No." I had come to terms with that fact years ago, which was why I was surprised at the ache I felt admitting it out loud. "I'd prefer not to talk about it, if you don't mind."

His eyes widened in surprise. At what, I didn't know. "Of course. I apologize if my questions upset you."

I expected for him to stay in the seat he was in, and that maybe we could chat or at least discuss the article I was to write. He didn't remain seated, though. After his unnecessary apology, he stood and walked back to the love seat where May sat. I couldn't tell if he sat down or not, and I wasn't about to turn and look over my shoulder at him. No way did I want either him or May to think I had any interest in what the two of them said or did.

But since I actually did, I strained my ears in order to hear what they were talking about. Unfortunately, between the low level hum of the aircraft, and the two assistants sitting on the other love seat, I couldn't hear a word from either Luca or May. In fact, I heard nothing from him for the rest of the flight.

CHAPTER 13

LUCA

THE PLANE WAS to land in Milan. May, Richard, and Wayne all had apartments in the city. Originally, I had requested for a hotel in the city to be booked for a reporter who was tagging along. The way I saw it, there was no need for them to be with me every second of the day, and I didn't want a stranger in my house.

All that changed when I discovered Wren was the reporter. I didn't want her in a hotel. I wanted her at my house. For multiple reasons. She'd shocked me with the leg injuries and the fact that she worked as a journalist. But if she thought she was the only one who had major life changes over the last few years, she was the one in for a shock.

Because I didn't want Carmella to know where Wren was staying, I had to work around her. I sure as hell didn't want her to know she would stay with me. I accepted the fact that I had a personnel problem when I couldn't ask my personal assistant to make hotel arrangements for me.

Carmella didn't know I'd met Wren the night of the reception and dinner that never happened. She was my PA, but that didn't give her unlimited access to my personal life. It was bad enough she knew Wren existed. There was no way possible I'd ever confide anything to her about my personal relationships. Much less one with all the emotional baggage my relationship with Wren held.

There was one thing I'd learned very early on about Carmella. She liked power. It didn't matter to her if she actually held that power, or if people only assumed she held it. They were both the same in her mind. When she had power, she thought she had something to hold over a person.

For the last few years as long as she did her job and did it well, I tried not to care how she got it done. But it was becoming all too clear that Carmella only did what Carmella wanted to do. I needed to let her go.

But I put it aside to deal with later.

When the plane landed, I made my way to Wren and slipped behind her.

"Wait," I said in a low voice, putting a hand on her shoulder.

She remained silent, but turned to look at me. I didn't miss the questions in her eyes. Instead of answering them, though, I looked toward my three employees and nodded, hoping she'd understand that I'd tell her more when we were alone.

I took her curt nod to mean she did, and we waited for them to disembark.

"What's going on?" she asked as soon as they left and we were alone.

"There's been a change in your itinerary," I told her.

She lifted an eyebrow. "Can we discuss it tomorrow? I'd like to just get to my hotel, take a shower, and grab some room service."

It wasn't until that moment I realized how my plan, which had sounded perfectly fine in my head, was going to sound when I said it out loud. My original idea, to tell her there'd been a change to where she'd be staying and that she would be at my house now, seemed too controlling and domineering. I couldn't imagine any woman, no matter who the guy was, would react positively toward being told that.

I tried my best to word it better. "The hotel room was booked before I knew you would be the reporter covering this story. But I was thinking since we know each other, you might be more comfortable at my house."

I paused to make sure she didn't plan to scream or hit me. Which would have been fine, considering. When she just looked at me and seemed to say go on with her expression, I continued, "It's a big house... more of an estate, really. Out near Como. And it's large enough so you wouldn't have to see me after hours if you didn't want. Plus, I think it'll be safer for you as well."

That last part wasn't a lie, not that the rest of what I said had been. But I'd made the reservation when I thought the reporter was a male. I knew it was perfectly acceptable for a woman to travel by herself. Call me old-fashioned, but I would feel better knowing Wren was under my protection than by herself at a cold and impersonal hotel.

"An estate? Near Como?" Wren asked. "You must do well for yourself. I mean, not like the private jet didn't tip me off, but I remember you being more of a city guy."

Which was true. I remembered talking with Wren about my plans to build my fashion empire in Milan and then move to New York City. I'd given no sign I had an interest in living anywhere other than a large city. But like Wren and her dance, life often took us on paths we never expected, much less planned for.

"I didn't buy the estate," I told her, not wanting to get into the details at the moment. Not until we were there, and maybe not until the next day, if possible. "It's more like a family property."

Her forehead wrinkled. "A family property? In Como. I thought your parents were from Rome?"

Of course she would have remembered that detail. Why would I have expected anything any different? She was a reporter. Details and remembering them were her job.

"It's a long story," I said, instead of answering her question directly. "I'll have to tell it to you." Later. Much later.

"I'll stay at your estate for tonight, and I'll see how I feel about it after that," Wren said.

It wasn't an enthusiastic agreement, but I hadn't expected one. I was thankful she hadn't demanded to be delivered immediately back to a hotel.

"One night," I repeated. "And if you wish to spend the rest of your time in Italy in a hotel, I will take you myself whenever you request."

By THE TIME we'd made it to the car I had waiting, it seemed Wren had been revitalized. Though in the jet, she'd announced her intention to spend her evening relaxing at and in her hotel room, I couldn't see her settling down anytime soon.

She appeared to have a goal of taking in everything she possibly could. It was almost as if I could see her brain working to catalogue every scrap of information she came across. There were a few moments scattered here and there while we waited for the car that Wren seemed to let her guard down. But only when she thought I wasn't watching. And in those moments, she reminded me so much of the Wren I remembered from the first day I saw her five years ago, it made my heart ache.

Was it the thrill of being in a new and different place? The excitement of a new country? I wasn't sure. I only knew it was impossible to keep my eyes off of her, so I had to watch her without her knowing I was watching.

"Remind me how far Como is from Milan," Wren requested as I followed her into the car.

"It'll take us about an hour to get there from here," I replied, and she nodded.

One hour.

Wren covered her secret with long skirts and pants, and she hadn't wanted to talk about it. I now knew exactly how she felt, except there was no way to cover my secret. And though I'd prefer not to discuss the topic, I now had an hour to decide how to do so.

CHAPTER 14

WREN

FRANKLY, I thought Luca was out of his mind to move from Italy to the US, and that was before we started on the drive from Milan to Como. How could anyone think about leaving this area and moving anywhere else? Much less to a place like Boston?

Not that I'd ever purposely wanted to bash my hometown, don't get me wrong. I love Boston. Being a reporter, I could choose to live anywhere I wanted, and I chose Boston. Even with the god-awful winters. But seriously, people, we're talking Italy for crying out loud.

The art. The history. The architecture. The landscapes. The food.

For Boston?

During my first, and only trip to Italy five years before, Luca and I had never ventured very far from the resort. He'd told me he'd grown up near Rome, and that most of his family still lived in that area. However, after college, and an apprenticeship, he'd moved to Milan.

We'd even made a vague sort of plan for him to show me the city of Milan when I returned. But, of course, those plans died along with the dreams of a career in ballet, days later on a darkened slope in Courmayeur. After that, I'd never thought that I'd ever return to the country, and I purposely avoided any and all things having to do with the area.

Driving along the road on the way from Milan to Como, there was no need, and no possible way to do so, even if I wanted. I tried to remember what, if anything, I knew about the Como area. Unfortunately, all I recalled was a long ago memory of seeing the name on a map and thinking it sounded kind of cool.

"What's Como like?" I asked Luca. Based on my estimate, we were about midway between Milan and our destination.

"Hmm?" He looked up from his phone.

Funny. Ever since we got into the car, he'd acted a bit off. And it seemed to me that he spent an inordinate about of time on his phone, texting.

"What's Como like?" I repeated.

His expression went blank for a minute. I could only guess he was trying to shift gears from the conversation he was having on his phone, and the one I had tried to start in person.

"Is everything okay?" I nodded at the phone he still had in his hands, thumbs ready to continue whatever he'd been in the middle of texting. "If there's an issue with something, or you need to go into work or anything, just let me know. I don't mind finding a taxi or something back to Milan."

That seemed to wake him up a bit. At least he set the phone down in his lap. "No," he said, and tucked the phone into the inner pocket inside his jacket. "Nothing of the sort. It's like I said, I thought the reporter was a male and had a hotel room booked. No one at the estate was expecting anyone other than me to arrive tonight. I had to ensure everything was in place for your arrival and to make sure preparations were made for your stay."

It all sounded good, but somehow his words and actions still seemed off. Or maybe it was more that they didn't match the other. His words seemed matter of fact and reasonable for our current situation, but for some reason, his body language spoke of unease.

I feared he didn't really want me at his estate. Maybe he'd only brought it up to be nice and hadn't thought that I'd actually take him up on his offer. That was why I'd given him an out and offered to stay at a hotel. I'd rather be at a hotel alone than to be at his estate because he felt an obligation to make the invitation.

Although, was it possible I would be that much of a bother? If you thought about it, I was one small person. How could my arrival put any kind of kink in the universe of an estate?

I tried not to think about it, but it was difficult. Luca didn't pull his phone back out, though based on the uncomfortable way he sat, it seemed he'd rather have it in his hand. I thought since he wasn't texting, he might try to start a conversation with me, or at least answer the question I'd asked him twice.

But he didn't. He sat and looked straight ahead. The longer we drove, the more uncomfortable he appeared to grow. He didn't have to speak a word for me to know something was on his mind. The only thing I could imagine it being was that perhaps the estate was run down or in the middle of being renovated. Maybe it was in such bad repair, it embarrassed Luca to have anyone see it. Though had that been the case, I wouldn't have imagined he'd have asked me to stay.

Since Luca wouldn't be forthcoming with any information about Como, I took in what I could with my observations alone. From what I gathered, Como was the name of the providence. There was a Como City, but we drove past that, following the shore of Lake Como. It wasn't until we passed a sign that simply stated "Laglio," that the car turned off the main road.

The area was breathtakingly beautiful, especially whenever I managed to catch a glimpse of the lake.

The car pulled up to a locked gate that opened once our driver entered a code. As we made our way onto the grounds of the estate, it hit me. Maybe Luca didn't want me on his estate, not because its condition embarrassed him, but because he thought I would find it pretentious.

At the sight of the main house, my jaw dropped. "Holy shit, Luca."

When he'd mentioned the estate was family property, and since I knew his family lived close to Rome, I'd assumed the estate was more of a vacation property. An idea that seemed even more probable considering the vicinity of Lake Como. But surely the massive home before me was more than a sometimes home to only visit occasionally.

The two-level home was constructed in white stone and surrounded by lush greens. Walkways and sculpted arches led to the sparkling lake beyond the main house.

I was still gaping at it when Luca helped me out of the car.

"It's gorgeous," I said. "And it's yours?"

He winced. "Not exactly."

I had no idea what that could mean. "I can't imagine leaving this for Boston."

Everything I saw looked so perfectly beautiful, I found it difficult to believe it was real. The house. The land. The gardens. They all belonged in a fairy tale, or at least a daydream.

"Can we go see the lake?" I asked. I was vaguely aware of our driver taking our luggage out of the car, and another man, who appeared to come out of nowhere, picking it up to carry inside.

"Yes," Luca said. "I just need to—"

His sentence was cut off by a child's high-pitched squeal. I turned toward the direction it came from and saw a small blur of white flying toward us. Behind the blur, in the middle of an open side door, stood a woman with an apologetic look on her face.

She looked a lot like Luca, was the only thought I could process before the blur came to a stop in front of him and wrapped her arms around his legs.

"Papa! Papa!" the dark-haired child, who couldn't be much over four, yelled. "You're finally home. What took so long? You were gone forever."

CHAPTER 15

I STARED at the young child in shock. *Papa?* Had she just called Luca, *Papa?*

He didn't look my way, but rather focused all his attention on the little girl, swinging her up in his arms in a big hug. "Gemma, *tesoro*. I'm sorry I was gone so long. I missed you so."

"You can't go away for such a long time ever again." She pulled her head back from where she had it buried in his chest and placed a small hand on each of his cheeks as she spoke. "Promise me, Papa."

"I'll do my best."

"Sorry, Luca." The woman who'd been standing in the doorway had made it to where we stood. "I tried to keep her with me until you made it inside, but as soon as she realized it was you, there was no stopping her."

"I'm a wiggly worm," Gemma said with a giggle and adding a demonstration, twisting this way and that. "See?"

"I see, *tesoro*." Luca kissed her cheek and still kept hold of her. "Have you been behaving for Auntie Maria?"

Auntie Maria. I'd thought the woman looked like Luca. She must be his sister. Where was the little girl's mother? Luca wasn't married, was he? How old was Gemma? Was she his daughter? I tried to do the math in my head, but I couldn't settle the questions in my head long enough to form an answer.

"Mostly." Gemma wrinkled her nose. "She told Grandmama that I was a handful, but she's wrong, isn't she, Papa? I'm two handfuls. It even takes you two hands to hold me."

Luca laughed in a way I'd never seen. "Yes, you're definitely two handfuls. Maybe three."

"Silly Papa. No one has three hands," she said, and then turned her head toward me, her eyes so similar to Luca's they took my breath. "Who are you?"

"This is Wren," Luca jumped in to answer, and I realized I'd been standing there, looking at the father and daughter in front of me. "She's from Boston, and she's going to write about our move."

"Hello, Wren," Gemma said. "My name is Gemma, I'm four, and I don't want to move to Boston." She turned her face back to Luca. "She can write that in her story."

"Hello, Gemma." I held out my hand, and she took it with a big smile and an exaggerated shake. "I'm Wren, and if I lived here, I wouldn't want to move to Boston, either."

Her eyes grew big. "Really?"

"Really," I replied.

Luca gave me a look I translated to mean, *you aren't helping*, but I didn't care. It was the truth. Besides, I had so many thoughts running around in my head, I didn't have the mental strength to use a filter.

Satisfied her papa was home, Gemma wiggled out of his arms, took a piece of chalk from a pocket in her dress, and starting drawing on the drive at our feet.

Luca asked his sister a question in hushed, rapid Italian. Was he trying to keep me or Gemma from overhearing? It wasn't clear. Not wanting to intrude, I turned my focus to Gemma's doodles.

I had little experience with children. I was an only child, and no one in my circle of friends or acquaintances had kids. They were like an exotic species to me, these little people.

And Luca had one.

I had so many unanswered questions, but only two I desperately wanted the answer for. Who and where was the child's mother? If Gemma was four, she was born after my disastrous ski trip. But her conception?

I wasn't a fertility expert by the stretch of anyone's imagination, but even I knew it fell close to my departure. Did that mean he'd been cheating on this mystery woman with me? The thought made my stomach turn.

Just as quickly as that question popped into my head, though, so did the realization that Luca had brought me here on purpose. And while Gemma's existence shocked me, Luca had known the entire time what he was doing. He'd known she'd be here, and he still canceled my hotel in order to ensure I would be as well.

He finished talking with his sister and then bent down to speak with Gemma. I watched as he interacted with his daughter and marveled at how he seemed an almost different man than the one I'd been around lately and more like I remembered him being years ago. He was animated, at ease. Free. Watching the duo made me smile. Especially how intently he listened as she explained what she'd drawn.

I felt the weight of someone watching and looked up to find his sister looking my way. She didn't appear abashed to be caught staring so brazenly, nor did she turn away. Instead, she smiled.

"How was your trip from Boston?" she asked. Her accent was much more pronounced than Luca's.

It wasn't until she asked me that my body realized how tired it was, and I found myself yawning at her question. I covered my mouth with my hand. "Sorry."

Maria laughed softly. "No apologies necessary. International travel always has the same effect on Luca."

She nodded toward where he and Gemma had moved a few steps down the drive. I turned and watched as Luca covered his own yawn.

"Are you tired, Papa?" Gemma asked. "It's not bedtime yet."

He stood up and took her hand. "No, but Papa didn't get a nap today."

Gemma apparently thought the idea of her father taking a nap was hilarious, because she laughed hard. "You don't take naps."

They had made it back to us, and I couldn't help but add, "He should have taken a nap. He was very grumpy on the plane."

Gemma looked at her father in surprise. He nodded. "I was. I won't say otherwise. But I'm home now with you, and I feel much better."

"Gemma," Maria said, holding out her hand. "Come with me and let Papa show Wren to her room. We'll get out the dinner we made for them and have everything set up so you can tell them how much you helped me prepare."

Gemma had taken her aunt's hand, and they were headed back to the side door they'd come out of, but Gemma turned for a second. "I had to show her how to do everything, Papa."

Luca smiled. "I can't wait to taste it."

We remained where we were, unmoving and silent until they entered the house. I broke the silence first.

"Your daughter is incredible, Luca," I said.

He continued watching the door they'd just entered. "Thank you. I've always thought so, but then again, I know I'm not the most unbiased person to ask."

Unsure about what to say or do, I did nothing.

"I'll sure you have a lot of questions, and I promise to answer them all," he said. "After Gemma goes to bed."

"I'm the one who sent you away and then left. You don't owe me any explanations, Luca." I'd realized as much when he acknowledged I had questions. Questions I had no right to have.

His somber gaze never left mine. "Don't I, though, Wren?"

CHAPTER 16

LUCA

Wren had been wrong to say I didn't owe her any explanations. I'd watched her do the math in her head when Gemma announced how old she was. It didn't take a mathematician to figure out the estimated timeline.

Wren turned away without responding to my question and walked toward the house. I shook my head. She might not think I owed her an explanation, but she was damn sure going to get one. Later, Gemma would be in bed and I could tell Wren about what happened to me after she left Italy.

First things first, though. I had to show Wren to the room that would be hers while she was here. After that, I'd show her around the estate a bit to give her a general idea of where everything was. The place was beautiful. It was also huge and had the capability of making one feel as if they needed a map to get around. Nearly every room and hallway in the maze of a house were white. I'd give Wren the high level tour today.

By the time we finished, it would be time to eat whatever Maria and Gemma had made for dinner. Gemma's bedtime would follow soon thereafter.

Like always, I smiled at the thought of Gemma. I had a few regrets in my life. Some bigger and potentially more far reaching than others, but my daughter was not one of them.

I turned to Wren. "Let me show you around."

I FOUND Wren in the library after I tucked Gemma into bed.

"That took longer than normal," I said in explanation. "I had to read two books instead of one because Gemma insinuated I didn't have a good dog voice. She said Auntie Maria's voice was better. I was left no choice by that point, but to read two books to prove the superiority of my dog voice." I wrinkled my forehead. "Although, now that I'm thinking back, she never gave me her final thoughts on the matter."

"Sounds to me she got what she wanted. An extra story read by her dad."

I snorted. "You're probably right."

Wren gave a smile of satisfaction, but remained silent. I could see the questions she had in her eyes. I also saw her determination not to ask a single one. But I knew what question had to be driving her crazy the most.

I took a picture frame from a nearby table and placed it in Wren's hands. Based on the way she sucked in a breath, she knew exactly who she was looking at.

"Her name was Gianna," I said. "She's Gemma's mother. She died soon after giving birth."

"Oh, Luca," Wren whispered. "I'm so sorry."

I sat down next to her. Close, but not close enough to touch. "Thank you," I said, determined to tell her the entire truth. "I appreciate that, but my relationship with her wasn't like that."

Wren raised an eyebrow, and I heard her unspoken question just as clear as if she'd asked it out loud, *If your relationship wasn't like that, how did you end up having a child together?*

"I grew up with Gianna." It was the best place to start, but I didn't add that Carmella was her best friend, or even that she still worked for me. There was something between Wren and Carmella. I wasn't sure what it was, and though I planned to get to the bottom of it and find out what it was, now wasn't the time. "And though we dated off and on for years, we knew the only thing between us was fun, and that we weren't soulmates or each other's better half."

Wren held herself still, almost as if she waited for the second shoe to drop.

"When I met you, Gianna and I had decided not to date because we worked better as friends than we did as lovers. After you left, I went a bit mad." I closed my eyes for a second hoping to block out feeling the overwhelming of sorrow and helplessness of that period of time. "I know you left instructions for me to let you go and not to attempt to find you, but I couldn't. Just like I couldn't forget you."

I risked a glance at her. I'm not sure what I expected to find in her expression, anger, maybe for not doing as she asked, but that wasn't what I found. Tears filled her eyes, threatening to fall with the slightest provocation. Seeing them made me forget what I'd been saying.

Because she wouldn't let me see her in the hospital and how quickly she'd left Italy, it'd always been my assumption our time together had meant more to me than it had to her. Now I wasn't so sure.

I cleared my throat and continued. "I hired private investigators and talked to anyone you'd talked to while you were in Italy. I thought if I searched long and hard enough, I'd eventually find you, but I didn't."

Wren wiped a tear from her face.

"About three months after you left, I had dinner with some friend and Gianna was there. A few days later, she came by my apartment in Milan. She'd just been dumped by her current boyfriend, and earlier in the day, I'd received a letter from the last investigator I had searching for you saying that he'd exhausted all leads. He couldn't find you and told me he wasn't looking any longer. I refused to listen to him, and he simply quit. It was later that night when Gianna showed up." I shook my head, remembering. "We were both upset and lonely. It wasn't the best reason for us to hook up for one last time that night, but it was good enough in the moment. She left the next morning, and to be honest, I'm not sure I thought about her afterward. I put all my time and energy into my business. That worked well until Gianna showed up again at my front door, two months later. She looked scared to death. That's when she told me she was pregnant.

Wren nodded, a silent plea for me to continue.

Picking up where I left off, I continued, "I offered to marry her, of course, but she would have nothing to do with that."

I remembered so vividly the weight in my stomach when I brought up the two of us getting married. My entire world had shifted in a matter of seconds, and all I could do was stand back and let it happen. Gianna would marry me and together we would raise our child. It was the honorable and right thing to do.

"I didn't believe her at first." I shook my head. "Damn. I was so full of myself back. I think I actually asked her if she had any clue as to what she was doing. She told me she did, and that she had more sense than to marry a man she didn't love."

"Ouch," Wren said.

I gave her a weak smile. "I'll admit, her words hit my pride right where it hurt the most."

"Let me see," Wren said. "I bet you saw yourself as a glorious white knight, riding in and saving the poor pregnant princess, and the only thing that happened was she knocked you right off the horse you rode up on."

"How did you know?"

She rolled her eyes. "Fucking men. You all think the same. I doubt any man has had a unique thought in at least fifty years or more."

I looked at her in shock.

"Believe it or not," she continued. "We don't always tell you things because we want or need you to fix them. Most of the time, we're just talking."

"I was trying to do the right thing," I insisted.

"Did you bring up getting married the same day she told you about the pregnancy?"

Of course. "Yes."

"Idiot," she whispered under her breath.

Instead of replying, I continued, "Gianna told me she had no desire to get married and that she wasn't sure how active a role she wanted me to take in everything. I suppose she still saw me as a playboy, even though she was the only woman I'd been with after you left." I didn't have to hear her comment to know what she was thinking. Five months without a hookup? Insert sarcastic wow. But for someone with my history of one night flings and a different woman on my arm whenever I went out, five months was huge. "I wasn't sure how she'd be able to raise a child alone. She had money and her parents' estate as part of her inheritance, but as for support people? There was no one."

"Wait," Wren said. "Her inheritance?"

"Yes. Her parents died in an accident right after she finished school." She nodded, and I continued. "As her pregnancy progressed, and I guess as she saw that I wasn't always out on the town, hunting for carnal pleasure, but instead spent my downtime being constructive, she changed her mind. She asked me to go with her to her doctor's appointment during her third trimester."

I'd never forget hearing Gemma's heartbeat for the first time. I had been standing next to the exam table Gianna occupied. A white sheet covered the swell of her belly. The day had already felt surreal. Ever since Gianna had gotten undressed and sat on the table, I'd watched in amazement the way my son or daughter would move, and how in doing so, made the thin sheet move as well.

That was the first time it truly hit me that we'd created another person. I sat in dumbstruck silence, content to watch the sheet move, while the doctor went about conducting his exam. When he'd announced he was going to check the baby's heart rate, I didn't know I'd be able to hear it. At first the strange staccato sound didn't resonate as my child's beating heart. Not until a worried Gianna asked if it was okay.

I was done for then. Between the movements of the sheet and the rapid beating of a tiny heart, my heart was filled with more love than I thought possible for it to hold. I was amazed at Gianna because until that moment, I had no idea how incredible the female body was. To have the ability to harbor and grow another complete human? How amazing was that?

For the span of about three minutes, I felt jealous. The only thing I did was produce sperm. Then the doctor began talking about birth plans and delivery options and it hit me that the growing baby had to come out somehow and I didn't see how that was in any way possible.

Suddenly, I wasn't jealous anymore. I was in complete awe.

But I didn't tell Wren all of that. Even though when it happened, the two of us weren't in a relationship, it was probably hard enough for her to see the proof that I'd been with another woman. I didn't need to talk about how amazing I thought her body was.

"Gianna was more receptive to me during those last three months," I explained to Wren. "We weren't romantically involved, but she at least put up with me being around." I stopped, knowing I had to go on, but dreading it as well.

Wren picked up on my hesitancy. She placed her hand on my arm. "What happened?"

I took a deep breath. "Gianna went into labor early. We made it to the hospital right as her water broke. For a while everything seemed normal, but as time went by and there was little progress, she started complaining that something wasn't right. Everyone kept saying she and the baby were fine. They gave her something to speed her labor up, and that seemed to help. But once it was time for her to push, she didn't have to say anything. I knew her well enough to see something was off, but she was completely focused on delivering."

I stopped to clear my throat and risked a peek at Wren. She wiped a tear from her cheek.

"Once things started happening, they hit so fast, it's all a blur looking back now. I heard a baby cry, someone said we a had a daughter, and Gianna crashed all in what felt like five seconds." I say anything else to spare her the details that still haunted me.

"Just that quickly," I said, jumping over the rest of Gemma's birth story. "Everything changed. I knew it would, of course. But I also counted on having Gianna to help. Going from directly from unattached bachelor to single dad was some kind of whiplash I'd never known existed."

Wren was silent, and I wished more than anything I could read her mind. What could be she be thinking?

I was getting ready to ask what was going through her head at the moment. Before I could get anything out, she smiled softly and shocked me by putting her hand on my knee. "Thank you for sharing that with me. I know it was difficult."

CHAPTER 17

WREN

THE NEXT FEW days were possibly the most unexpected ones I'd had since the last time I was in Italy. Though I was supposed to be on assignment, this job was nothing like any I'd ever experienced.

A human interest story on an international business owner moving from Italy to the States wasn't all that interesting. I sat in on a few of Luca's meetings and there was nothing newsworthy in any of them. Not with the content, anyway. If I wrote an article using the notes I'd taken during those meetings, no doubt I'd be let go for writing the most boring thing to ever be put on paper.

But if I looked outside the content of the meetings, now there was a human interest story. The single dad, on the cusp of making it big in the fashion industry while trying to move everything over the sea to America? One hundred eighty degrees from boring.

He held most of his meetings at the estate. One entire wing was dedicated to his business, including what had to be the world's biggest office. Or at least it was the biggest I'd ever seen. He only used half of it, I soon discovered. The other half was Gemma's.

"I had to do it," he said when I asked about the unconventional office setup. "I had to work, but I didn't want to be away from Gemma. She's already lost her mother, she won't lose her father to his job."

I learned what it meant when he'd said the estate was family property. It had been in Gianna's family and passed to her upon the death of her parents. Being as young as she was, Gianna didn't have a will. From what I gathered from some of the household staff, Luca had spent a fortune ensuring everything including the estate was put in trust for Gemma. Technically, I suppose, one could say he was living at his daughter's estate.

Two days after landing in Italy, I realized I was in deep trouble. Before, at the skiing resort, Luca was an intelligent, charming, and good-looking guy who caught my eye. Now, he was much more dangerous. That guy had grown to be a man who'd held the responsibly of both business and family. One he'd chosen and wouldn't leave. The other had been a surprise he now couldn't live without.

In short, being around him for any length of time put me in danger of losing even more of my heart to him.

It was midafternoon and Gemma was down for her nap. Luca had left for Milan before breakfast to finish some paperwork that had to be signed and delivered in person. He said it was better for him to leave in the morning because he'd be home early enough to spend time with Gemma.

I'd decided to let him go without me. There was nothing more boring than paperwork, and I had no desire to sit around and watch Luca take care of it. Talk about a major snooze fest. Regardless, I'd yet to check in with Zach, and I knew he was eager to hear how things were going. Or so I guessed from the handful of emails he'd sent with the subject I NEED A STATUS UPDATE. Just like that, both bolded and in all caps.

Since he'd decided I was single and had all this free time with no commitments, and therefore it was no hardship for me fly out of the country at the drop of a hat, I decided he, being neither single nor without commitments, didn't have time to read a status update. I'd put it off for two days and I was certain in Zach's mind that was one and a half days too long.

Or that had been my plan.

What ended up happening was that after breakfast Gemma wanted to show me her favorite outside hiding place. I'd discovered on my first day it was nearly impossible to tell the little girl no, so less than fifteen minutes after putting our breakfast dishes in the sink, Maria and I found ourselves outside with Gemma dressed in the cutest dress/costume and looking like a fairy princess.

The outfit was gorgeous. I'd seen nothing like it before.

"Come on," Gemma said, grabbing my hand and pulling me toward the all white flower garden. "It's in here."

In the middle of the garden was a pink child-sized tent, large enough for Gemma to crawl into, but no one who was near adult-sized. Not that I need worry. As soon as Gemma scooted inside, she was right back outside, holding a pink blanket.

"Here," she said. "You can sit on this."

Needless to say, I spent most of my day hunting for fairies in the garden with Maria and Gemma not so much on my STATUS UPDATE, much to the annoyance of Zach, or so I hoped. Once Gemma went down, I decided I should drop him a line, though, so at least he knew I was alive. I'd just typed a short and vague I'm here, everything's fine, and the article is coming along great note, and hit send, when Luca walked into the sunroom.

"Working?" he asked.

I closed my laptop. "Just finished. You?"

"Yes. Finally." He sat down on one of the room's couches. "I heard from Maria that you spent your morning with Gemma."

"Yes," I replied. "She's delightful."

He smiled. "She is. But I know she can also be exhausting. I don't want you to feel as if you have to give into her every whim. Believe it or not, she has been told no before, and I'm aware you're not here on vacation or to babysit."

"She's fine, really," I said. "And I don't want to come across as condescending, but you've done a superb job raising her."

"Thank you." He nodded. "But I can't take all the credit. Maria has helped a lot."

I had wondered about that. She didn't live at the estate, but she had a bedroom here, and she'd spent the night both nights that I had been here. She was very much like her younger brother, witty and charming with a laugh that came easily.

"Does she stay here a lot?" I asked.

"Not usually," Luca said. "She comes over and stays with Gemma when I have to travel for work, but fortunately, that hasn't happened much, believe it or not. I'm usually able to get what I need to get done from my office."

"I would hope so," I said. "It's certainly big enough."

He laughed, and for the two thousandth time I wondered how in the world Tenor had ever thought he was boring. With that thought, I remembered I probably needed to touch base with Mia. Unlike Zach, however, I had sent her a few texts and pictures. Though I hadn't yet told her about Gemma.

"If you're wondering why Maria's been staying, even though I'm back—" he started.

"No, it's none of my business," I hurried to stop him. "I assumed it was to watch Gemma while you work."

He still wore his smile. "That's only a tiny part. She's mainly here because of you."

I felt my face flush. "Why? Does she know about our past? Or is she afraid I've come from America to Italy in order to steal your virtue?"

He laughed hard at that. "I'm pretty sure she knows me well enough to know that I have no virtue left to steal. I had a child out of wedlock, you know? No, she's staying to ensure I don't steal your virtue."

I swallowed hard. "I didn't realize it was in danger."

His gaze seemed to penetrate straight to my soul. "You should know me well enough to realize I want more than your virtue. I want all of you."

He stood up and walked to the couch I was sitting on and sat down beside me. "The question is, do you want me?"

It was a ridiculous question. Of course I wanted him. I'd wanted him since the day we met in Italy. But wanting and having are two very separate things.

"It doesn't matter what I want," I told him. "I'm here to observe and interview you in order to write an article. Anything else would be considered out-of-scope."

"Out of scope?" He cocked an eyebrow at me. "Are we negotiating something I was unaware of? Because what I have in mind has nothing to do with business."

Not only do I want him, but I realize at that moment that I'm going to do something about it. I leaned closer to him and dropped my voice. "Whatever did you have in mind?"

He sucked in a breath, and I could tell my reply was the last thing he expected. The knowledge emboldended me. I ran a finger down the broad expanse of his chest. He didn't have a suit on at that moment. He must have changed when he got home. The navy tee shirt he'd put on made it much easier to see his body react to my touch.

"You keep touching me like you are, and you'll find out pretty quickly," he said in a half threat, half promise.

"Really?" I asked. "What would your sister think about your plans?"

"For fuck's sake, don't mention my sister," he said.

"Does your sister normally cock block you?"

"Please for the love of God, don't use the words sister and cock in the same sentence."

I laughed at his unease and he glared at me like he was mad, but I knew wasn't.

"Come here," he said, pulling me into his arms, where I went willingly.

Right before our lips touched, someone called down the hall for him.

"Luca?" they asked again and we both realized at the same time it was Maria.

Luca buried his head in my chest with a moan.

I stroked his hair. It seemed to be thicker than I remembered, and my mind wandered to other parts of his body and how they might have changed.

"Luca?" Maira called again.

I push him up and away. "You better go see what she needs before she finds you in here trying to take my virtue. Because she'll never leave us alone if she sees us like this."

He stands with a sigh and straightens his clothes.

"Can I call her a cock blocker now?" I asked.

He took one of my hands and brought it to his mouth to place a soft kiss on it. "If you come to my room after Gemma is down for the night, I'll let you do damn near anything."

CHAPTER 18

WREN

THE REST of the day passed way too slow. I made a few more notes and even attempted to outline the article. I totally sucked at outlines and the one I made for the article was no different. I thought about deleting it and starting over because I was pretty sure Zach would hate the direction I was taking the article, but I stopped myself before hitting SEND. If he asked, I'd send it then, but until he did, he wasn't getting anything from me.

Late in the afternoon, I saw where Zach replied to my email. I opened it on my phone to read, but saw he'd written a freaking novel. I didn't even attempt to skim the thing, but instead clicked out. His rambling ass could be dealt with later. Especially since I'd already made my mind up about turning in my notice.

Night had fallen, and Gemma had been in bed for about an hour, I'd held off walking the halls toward Luca's room because I wasn't sure where Maria was. I told myself it shouldn't matter what his older sister thought about me visiting Luca's room, any time I felt like doing so. But the truth was, it did matter.

Luca was obviously very close to his sister, and his sister was an integral part of Gemma's life. Even though I was merely passing through, I didn't want to cause any waves between the two siblings.

When I decided enough time had passed and that surely Maria had settled into whatever activity she had planned for the evening, I stepped out into the hallway.

Though the estate house was massive, I'd soon learned it had a very well thought-out floor plan. All the bedrooms were in one wing, Luca's business took up another, one held what I considered to be common areas, living and dining rooms, and the fourth was actually an outside space, partially covered and offering breathtaking views of the water beyond. My room was on the second floor, complete with my own private bathroom and a deck overlooking the lake. Luca, Gemma, and Maira were located downstairs.

I closed the door behind me so it appeared as if I was inside sleeping. Not that anyone would check, I told myself. Seriously, it wasn't like the housekeeper would come by and need me for anything, and though Maira and I got along, we weren't on close enough terms to warrant her making a midnight visit to my room.

Even so, I let out a deep breath of relief when I tiptoed by her door and saw it was closed. There was a light on, visible under her door, but then again, it was early enough that I hadn't expected her to be in bed.

I had walked by Luca's bedroom on the first day of my arrival, so I knew it wasn't far from either Maira or Gemma's. His door was cracked open and as I walked by, he reached from behind and pulled me inside. I didn't have a chance to catch my breath before he closed the door and pressed my back against it.

"What took you so long?" His breath heated my skin as he whispered along the lines of my neck.

I tilted my head to the side, allowing him better access. "I wanted to make sure no one saw me."

"Why would anyone care?"

"Based on what you told me earlier about your sister, I thought she might have a care or two."

It didn't appear as if he heard me. His lips made a hot trail from my neck to my lips, where he teased me with tiny kisses and seductive nibbles.

He tried to pull back and chuckled when I wouldn't let him budge an inch. "I thought you wanted to ensure we weren't caught?"

I clutched his shirt in my hands. "It's a risk I'll take."

"No," he said. "You were right. We shouldn't do this here."

I loosened my grip. "But we can do it somewhere?"

He laughed and held out his hand for mine. "Come with me, I know just the place."

I took the offered hand and allowed him to lead me through his room to the large glass doors in the back. I wondered how many women he'd he done this with.

"And take that look off your face," he added before I could say anything.

"What look?"

"The one calculating the number of women I've brought here."

My cheeks heated. "I wasn't aware my thoughts were so transparent."

"Your poker face is essentially nonexistent." He came to a stop before the glass door and caught my gaze. "And totally unneeded in this instance. I've never brought a woman here."

A small gasp escaped my mouth before I could stop it. A gasp that didn't go unnoticed by him.

"Now," he said. "Do you want to see what I had in mind?"

His revelation stunned me. He'd never brought a woman here? "Yes," I replied. "But can I technically be considered a woman you brought here since I'm here on business?"

His eyes darkened. "I cancelled your hotel room, didn't I?"

I looked into his eyes, and it suddenly hit me, I didn't care how the two of us got to the point we were currently at. Nor did I care who knew where I was or what I was doing. I dropped his hand.

"No," I said.

He looked confounded. "I apologize if my affections were unwanted. I meant no disrespect."

I blinked at him, trying to figure out what he was apologizing for, and when it hit me, I felt like an idiot.

"Sorry, I didn't mean no to you," I said. "And I really didn't mean to confuse you. It all made sense in my head, so I spoke without thinking."

He still looked confused, and I mumbled a curse, hoping I hadn't ruined the entire night. "What I was saying no to was for us to leave your room and go somewhere else. I want to stay here, in this room, and I don't care who knows."

His expression dissolved into a big grin that covered his entire face. "Thank God."

I giggled a bit. Probably because of nerves, but also because of the misunderstanding. "Did you think I was going to say no to tonight?"

"I'm not sure what I thought, to be honest. I only knew that no wasn't a word I expected, and it shocked the hell out of me." He cocked an eyebrow at me. "Come here."

He didn't have to tell me twice. We might have not been very far away, but there was more distance between us than either one of us wanted. In less than a second, I was in his arms and he was kissing me again.

"My sister is right next door," he said in between kisses.

"I don't care," was my reply.

My body felt alive for the first time in years. Even in his hotel room the night of our disastrous date, I hadn't felt like this. For tonight, and for as long as my time in Italy would allow, I'd be the woman I used to be. The woman before the accident. The one Luca remembered.

There would never be an us. We had too much history behind us, and he had a daughter. I could accept that. And I knew it would hurt like hell when it was over, but screw it, I'd been through leaving him once before and lived through it. It'd be hard, but I knew I could do it.

For this little bit of time, I'd pretend.

"Where did you go?" he whispered.

I shouldn't have been surprised he could read my body and mind as accurately as he could. For whatever reason, we'd always seemed to be acutely aware of the other. Or at least that was the case five years ago.

"Just lost inside my mind," I assured him. "Nothing really."

"None of that tonight, *vita mia*," he said. "No need to think of anything other than the pleasure I give you. Let me."

"Yes." For years I'd denied myself the freedom to remember how well he could give me pleasure. But at his request and at my one word acceptance, the rush of it all came back. The newly revived part of me relished the sensual being I became in his arms.

I was hungry for his touch and like a starving woman, I bared both body and soul to him. With swift and knowledgeable fingers, he made quick work of my clothes. Yet even his fervor was tempered to ensure he gave as much, if not more, than he received.

"You're so beautiful," he said almost reverently when I stood naked before him. "So much more so than I remember."

For the first time in years, hearing his words, I felt beautiful. True beauty, though, and not beauty as defined by the world. The beautiful he made me wasn't based upon what I looked like, how toned I was at the moment, or whether my legs were a scarred mess. I was beautiful because with him, I allowed myself to be the woman I always wanted to be. With him, I allowed myself to be free.

It was a freedom that empowered me and made me bold. I started with the shirt buttons at his neck and worked my way down. I made certain to try my best not to allow my fingers to touch his skin at all. I knew how much I wanted to touch him, to feel him under my hands, and I assumed he would feel the same, if not more so.

I glanced up from working on his buttons. He was breathing heavily, so heavily it made his nostrils flare. His eyes were dark and hooded. He was hanging on by a string, and that string was unraveling right before my eyes.

I finished with the buttons and pushed the shirt off his shoulders. He twisted and shrugged his arms out of it until it dropped to the floor. The entire time he kept his gaze locked on mine. I dropped my eyes only once he was shirtless before me, so I could get his pants off even slower.

But as soon as I reached for the button at his waist, his hands covered mind.

"Better let me," he said in a gruff voice I didn't recognize. "If you touch me once, I fear our first time tonight will be over before it starts."

That was the power he allowed me to have, and that power gave me a confidence I'd never experienced and one I'd never hoped to hold. Like a flower, I bloomed for Luca.

And I hoped that when I was no longer in his light, that I'd somehow keep myself from wilting back down and into who I'd become over the last few years.

CHAPTER 19

LUCA

I wasn't sure what had changed in Wren's mind since the last time we were in a similar situation, but I was grateful for whatever it was. Maybe she finally saw herself the way I saw her and realized her scars didn't bother me.

I'd wanted to rip her clothes off and have her naked in under sixty seconds, but I refrained. I tempered my urge, and managed to drag it out maybe a little more than a minute, but not much. However, I couldn't congratulate myself on my restraint, because as soon as the last piece of her clothing hit the floor, she reached for me.

Five years ago, I'd spent who knew how many hours after Wren left, trying to recall what her touch felt like. Though I'd thought I'd remembered, once she started undoing my shirt buttons and her fingers brushed my bare skin, I knew my memories hadn't come close.

The corner of my mouth lifted when I realized she was trying her best not to touch me. The little tease. I'd have to make sure I paid her back for that. Eventually. For the moment, I kept my moans to myself and let her continue with my shirt. All that changed, however, once my shirt hit the floor, and she reached for my pants. As much as I hated to do so, I had to stop her. If she touched me below the waist, I'd lose it like a teenaged boy.

She pouted, but relented and moved her hand. I loved how she wasn't bashful around me. After she ran out because of her insecurities about her legs, I'd feared she'd be hesitant if we were ever again in a similar situation. A misplaced fear based on her current behavior.

She took a slight step back. Enough room for me to handle the job of removing my pants and for her to watch, but no more.

"Moving awful slow there," she teased. "I'm growing older by the second."

"Sorry," I said, feeling playful. "Did you say something? I was admiring the view."

She put her hand on her hip. "If you don't get busy taking those pants off, I'll do it for you, and damn the consequences."

She would too. There wasn't a doubt in my mind she'd do that exact thing, and while I would enjoy every second, I hadn't been lying about how close I teetered on the edge. I'd be damned if our night would end this early. I had major plans for Wren once I had her back in my bed. Plans I wouldn't let her goad me into revising.

"I'll take them off." I undid the button at my waist. "But you have to watch."

"Do I look like I'm getting ready to run off somewhere?" She asked, and the vision of Wren running up and down the halls of the estate were so vivid in my mind, I had to smile.

"Not at the moment," I said.

"Then get busy."

Though our time together before had been unforgettable, it had occurred over five years ago. While there were moments of those few days I could recall with vivid clarity, there was no way for one to remember every second of those days five years later. It saddened me there were moments time had allowed to slip from my memory. Yet I had to admit, it was pure delight to discover new things about the woman I'd known so intimately so many years ago.

"Have you always been this bossy?" I smiled as worked my zipper down. "Because I don't remember you being this forceful. I think it's hot."

She arched an eyebrow, insinuating, I supposed, that she didn't believe me.

I chuckled. "Trust me, the way I see it, there is nothing hotter than a woman who knows what she wants and isn't afraid to let anyone know." I pulled down both my pants and boxer briefs at the same time and took a step out of them. "Tell me, Wren. What do you want?"

Her gaze hadn't dropped from mine while I was taking my pants off, but after hearing my question, her eyes went straight to my cock.

"You," she said in a raspy voice.

I took myself in my hand. "This part, too?"

"Hell, yes," she said, licking her lips, and I swore I grew harder. "Especially that part. What I really want is to taste that particular part. I'd lick the tip, swirl my tongue around the little slit, and then I'd take all of you in my mouth at once, letting you fuck yourself into my throat. "

Fuck, she didn't have to touch me. I'd wager anything, she could make me lose my shit with her words alone. Her words painted a picture of her doing exactly what she said she wanted to do. Hearing her talk about it made me almost spill into my hand, so I let go of my cock for fear my own touch would set me off. I took a deep breath and shoved the image of her on her knees, sucking me off out of my mind. Or I tried, anyway.

"I'd like nothing more than to give you the taste you want," I assured her, and even to my own ears, my voice was rough. "And maybe we can do that later, but for now, you'll have to wait."

Acting as if she'd spent countless hours in my room, and this wasn't the first time she'd been inside, she strolled to my bed and climbed on, settling herself on her back. "I guess I can wait." Her hand drifted between her legs. "As long as you don't make me wait too long."

As enjoyable as it would be to sit back and watch as Wren pleasured herself, the only orgasms she'd get tonight would be from me.

I didn't reply, but walked to the bed and climbed on top. Seeing her there on my bed, spread and needy for me, made me feel like I was king of the world. Hell, forget that, with her in my bed, I was the fucking king of the world.

Though damn near every cell in my body protested, I wouldn't take her yet. I situated myself between her legs and smiled up at her. "Get comfortable," I told her.

She flopped back onto the bed with a moan.

"Oh yes, *vita mia*," I said. "I have you exactly where I want you, and I'm not moving until you've come at least twice."

I had hoped that focusing on Wren and her pleasure would help me step away from the edge. That bringing her multiple orgasms would enable me to calm my own need a bit. However, I soon found the longer I spent teasing her wasn't doing anything but heightening my arousal.

My exploration of her body, remembering what once brought her the most pleasure, and doing it now to see if it still did, resulted in the sweetest rewards possible- her blissful sighs and moans. Unfortunately, while they were what I was after, they did nothing to relieve or lessen my desire for her. Instead, all they did was stoke it.

I'd vowed that she'd come twice before I moved. Therefore, even though my dick thought it was in charge, it was wrong. It wouldn't be getting its way until I did what I said I would.

"Now," Wren said, tugging at my shoulders and attempting to pull me up after her second release. She'd been wonderfully responsive years before, and she was even more so now. It hadn't taken very long at all to make her come twice. And for that, I was eternally grateful. I could have continued relearning her, but I was more than ready to get inside her.

"So bossy," I said, attempting to act indifferent, but falling miserably short of being able to carry it off. No doubt, she could see through me as if I were made of nothing except glass. But she didn't appear to see the need to call me out on it. Either that or she didn't want to waste time doing so. I was fine with either.

I ran my nose up along the inside of her leg, inhaling her intoxicating scent, a combination of her floral body wash, and her own unique smell. Unable to stop myself from doing so, I went back down her leg so I could go back up, but tasting her the second time. When I pretended I would do it a third time, she wrapped herself around me in an attempt to keep me from moving.

"No," she said, tightening her legs around me. "Now. Fuck me now, damn it."

I loved how feisty she became when she was aroused. Who knew something like that could turn me on even more?

Although I was beginning to think everything about Wren turned me on.

"I can't do anything with you wrapped around me like this," I said, pointing to how her arms and legs still held me immobile. She might not be dancing anymore, but she was doing something to stay in shape. Her legs were almost viselike the way they squeezed my body.

She looked in my eyes and there was no denying the need and desire I saw in their depths. "If I let you go, you have to promise you won't do anything other than fuck me," she said.

"You drive a hard bargain, *vita mia.*"

"I'm more interested int the hard things you can drive," she said, untangling herself from me and letting me move.

"Do you want to see exactly how hard I can drive things?" I drew myself up to my knees in between her parted legs.

"Yes," was all she said.

I ran a hand down each of her legs one at a time, watching her face as I did so. She didn't walk or move with any type of impediment, but I didn't know enough details about her injury to know what may or may not cause pain or discomfort. And I'd be damned if she'd experience either in my bed. "Let me know if this hurts or is uncomfortable."

She nodded, but said nothing. I wasn't sure if that meant she thought there could be a potential of either, if she was placating me, or if I was simply reading too much into the situation.

"I'm good with whatever you have in mind," she whispered.

"Promises. Promises," I said. "You don't know what things might be going on inside my mind."

"I'm willing to take that chance." Her eyes danced with mischief. "Try me."

I kept watching her as I lifted first one leg and then the other over my shoulder, spreading her even wider for me. She let out a moan, but it was one of pleasure and not distress.

"Still okay?" I asked, anyway.

"I'm not a fragile doll, Luca." Her voice held no anger, but was insistent all the same. "I promise I won't break when you touch me."

"You do realize I'm getting ready to do a hell of a lot more than touch you, right?" To drive her even more crazy, I rubbed my dick along her wet slit, but didn't thrust yet.

"You better be," she said with a mock eye roll. "Though the way you keep jabbering on and on makes me wonder if there's any action buried underneath all that talk?"

I couldn't stop my laugh. I didn't remember sex being so fun. "You're asking for it now."

"Yeah. Yeah. Yeah. So you keep saying. I've yet to experience anything other than talk."

"What about the two orgasms you had? You haven't forgotten those, have you?"

She arched an eyebrow. "What orgasms?"

And then, just because it was what she least expected, I lined myself up and gave her exactly what she'd asked for.

CHAPTER 20

WREN

The teasing follow up I had to my what orgasm question died on my lips as Luca entered me with one hard thrust.

"Holy fucking shit," I said, trying to blink away the stars from out of my eyes.

He'd held still, buried deep inside me, and knew it had to pure hell for him. I squeezed my muscles around him and his eyes rolled back. "Don't... fuck...." He took a deep breath. "I'm holding on by a thread."

"Me, too."

"I'm not going to last," he warned.

"I don't care," I panted. "I'm not either."

"Fast this time and slower the next?"

I shifted my hips forward, desperately trying to get him deeper. "Yes, damn it. Just move."

He caught my gaze and based on the mischief I saw dancing in the depths of his eyes, I assumed he'd hold still for longer just because I asked him not to. But all at once, the corner of his mouth lifted up, and I had just enough time to grab hold of the sheets at my side before he pulled out and slammed back into me.

Again.

And again.

"Like this?" he asked, thrusting again.

With my legs over his shoulders, he went deep, hitting spots inside me I didn't know existed. I hadn't been stretching the truth when I told him how close to release I was. The way he worked his cock soon had me panting.

"So good," he said, keeping his rhythm steady. "So fucking good."

It was too much. Watching him above me, the strain of his muscles as his body worked in and out of mine.

"I'm so close," I moaned. "Harder. Do it harder."

He increased the strength of his thrust. "Squeeze my dick like before." I tightened myself around him when he pulled out. "Yes. Fuck yes."

With his next thrust, he went deeper, and I was done for. My third orgasm hit hard and fast. Luca mumbled something under his breath, pumped his hips one last time and his release followed.

We stayed entwined for several long moments as our breathing and heart rates returned to normal. I remembered this. Those moments composed of both the satisfied bliss of *after* and the building anticipation of *again*.

Luca sat up with a moan and left the bed only long enough to dispose of the condom. I rolled over to my side to watch him as he walked naked across the floor. After he crawled back under the covers, he pulled me close.

"I remember us being good together, but I don't remember us being *that* good," he whispered in my ear.

I had to admit I felt the same way. "Do you think it's because we're older and wiser?"

"Me, personally?" he asked. "I think it was because I've been without you for so long."

"Mmm."

He raised an eyebrow. "What do you think it was?"

"I'm not sure," I said, trying to make my voice as serious as possible. "But I'm not sure it was all that much better."

"You're not?" His genuine worry proved I'd carried off the serious tone.

"No," I said. "We definitely should repeat it so we can know with certainty."

He grinned. "I'm all for that, but this time we're going to go slower."

"Slow's good," I agreed. "That'll make it easy for us to confirm we're better together now."

THAT'S WHAT WE DID. With the urgency of the first time behind us, we each wanted to spend more time on the second. Drawing out our touches and kisses. Relearning the other person and discovering new things about them. We consumed each other with our senses. Taste. Touch. Sound.

We hadn't discussed tomorrow or the next day or the week after that. There were no promises asked for, and none had been given. Neither of us knew how things would go between us, or if we even wanted them to go anywhere.

There were conversations that needed to happen and things that had to be brought up.

Not tonight.

I told myself tonight was for me. I'd lost a lot in the last five years, and if I had to give up more, so be it. But tonight was mine.

Mine and his.

Ours.

CHAPTER 21

WREN

Two DAYS LATER, I sat by the estate's outdoor pool while I sorted and organized my notes. I had enough to draft the first part of the article. My goal was to have the piece completed by the time we touched down in Boston. The way I saw it, the sooner I turned it in, the sooner I could resign.

I heard Luca's voice from what sounded like a fairly good distance away. I took a quick peek and saw he was on the phone, pacing along the outside deck area of the business wing. He was dressed casually, at least for him, a pair of khaki pants and a white button-down shirt with the sleeves folded up to the elbows. It shouldn't be legal for a man with his body and muscle tone to wear anything that displayed his arms so well. I found it hard to look at anything else.

My face heated as I remembered how those arms felt wrapped around me the night before last. And once that memory came to mind, other similar ones joined. How he'd taken his time to pleasure me, even though it was clear his control was at the edge of its breaking point. Our teasing banter in bed. The intensity of him thrusting into me. The way we stayed entwined with each other for a brief rest before doing it all again.

I spent most of the night in his bed. Luca had asked me to stay the entire night, but I didn't want to be caught in his bedroom. As far as the house staff knew, I was only a reporter. Maria might have known about our past, but it wasn't from my lips. So, around four thirty, I made my way back into my room, unnoticed.

Luca told me before I left that he'd come to my room next. Unfortunately, Gemma started vomiting not long after lunch, and when night fell, she only wanted to sleep in Luca's bed.

Needless to say, he never made it to my room.

I was watching him pace, wondering what could have him so aggravated, when I heard a small, "hello," from behind me.

I turned to find Gemma. Her cheeks had more color than the day before, and she was smiling. Her outfit was once again gorgeous. It looked like a short princess gown with a tutu. It sounded horrible described in my head, which was a shame because it was quite lovely.

"Hi, Gemma," I said. "You look like you feel better."

"I do," she said, but then crossed her arms and stuck out her bottom lip. "But Daddy said I can't go to dance class today because I throwed up so much yesterday."

"That actually sounds like a good idea," I said.

"It does?" she scrunched up her nose. "Why?"

"I can think of two reasons," I said. "One, you may still have some of the germs that made you sick, and if someone stood next to you, they could get the germ from you, and then they might get sick next."

"Okay," she said with a nod, but looking like she didn't believe a word I said. "What's number two?"

"Number two is that even though you feel fine, your body may need more time to heal. If you push yourself too hard or too fast, you might get even sicker. And that would mean even more missed dance class."

Gemma's reply was a yawn.

"See?" I said. "You're yawning. That proves you need to rest today."

"No," she said. "I'm yawning because Daddy snores so loud, I couldn't sleep last night."

"Are you telling Wren our family secrets?" Luca said.

I looked to my side and found him walking down the path from his office space to the pool. He wasn't talking on the phone, but there was something lingering in his eyes.

"No, Daddy," Gemma said. "I was talking about how loud you snore. So loud you keep me awake all the time."

Luca chuckled. "Does that mean you're moving back to your own bed tonight?"

"Yes. When I'm in my room, I can't hear all the snoring you do."

"Gemma!" Maria appeared over on the other side of the pool. "Come back over here. I told you not to wear that outside."

Gemma wrapped her around her body. "But I love it. It's pink and has a tutu. And Daddy made it specially for me."

I was pretty certain my mouth hit the ground. Obviously, I knew what Luca did, who he was. Heck, I'd even visited some of his designs in a few of the high-end stores in Boston. Yet, it never occurred to me that he'd use his talent for anything other than women's fashion. Stupid, I know.

"You made those outfits?" I asked, watching Gemma twirl on her tippy toes back to Maria.

"Not all of her clothes," Luca said.

"But that one and the one she wore that first day in the garden?"

He nodded, like it was nothing.

"They're fabulous, Luca," I said, unable to keep the admiration from my voice.

"It's just a little something I do on the side for Gemma."

"What?" I asked. "You don't sell them?"

He raised an eyebrow at me. "No. I design women's clothing. Not children's."

"Not to knock your women's stuff because I've seen it, and it's very nice. Wonderful even, but Luca, what you do for Gemma is magical."

He seemed to think about that. "I know nothing about the clothing market for children. Maybe if I didn't have this move to the US hanging over my head, I could look into it more."

His words shocked me. I'd been assuming he was the one who wanted to move to the States. But to hear what he'd just said, I wasn't sure. "Move to the US hanging over his head," didn't sound like someone who was looking forward to the change.

"Why are you moving?" I asked. Why hadn't I asked him before?

"I want to show you something. Walk with me," he said, and nodded toward the path leading to Lake Como. I stood, and we started walking.

He continued talking, "My advisors encouraged me to make the move. They thought overall it would be better off for the company."

"The company meaning you and your designs?"

"Yes. I also thought it might be more advantageous for Gemma to grow up in the US. So the decision really made itself."

We walked along the edge of the lake, a gentle breeze rustled our hair.

I tucked a wayward strand behind my ear. "If you could do anything you wanted, would you move to the States?"

He took a long moment, pondering, or maybe searching for the right words. "It's not that I don't want to move. It's that we're going to be leaving so much behind. This estate is Gemma's, and you heard her on your first day here. She doesn't want to move."

"I can't say that I blame her," I said. "It'd take a lot for me to leave this place."

"Maria will be heartbroken as well," he added.

"She isn't going with you?" I was surprised. My assumption had been that she'd be moving along with them. Though I wasn't sure why I thought that.

"I asked her to move with us," he said. "But she said the only reason she'd go would be for Gemma, and I can't ask her give up her life for her niece." He shot me a knowing grin. "Plus, there's a guy who lives in Como that wants to marry her, and I think she'd say yes if she wasn't afraid she'd be leaving me in a mess. She won't listen to me when I tell her Gemma and I would be fine. If we stay, I'm afraid she'd still be giving up her life."

He was silent for a few moments before turning, and I realized we weren't walking toward the lake like I thought we were but heading toward the business wing of the estate.

"Looked like a pretty intense phone call you were on earlier," I said.

He nodded. "Yes. In fact, the entire move might be in jeopardy."

It shocked me he looked as calm as he did. "Why?"

"Cost." He snorted. "Isn't that what it always is? I knew it would be ridiculously expensive, but I hadn't anticipated just how much ridiculousness was possible."

"You don't look overly concerned," I said.

"And I should be, right?" he asked. "That's what one would normally do if something one had been working on for over a year appeared to be on the verge of falling apart."

Duh, I wanted to say, but kept silent.

"I told the head of the board that I'd think over my options and have an answer for him in twenty-four hours."

"That fast?" I asked.

"It's the only way to plug the hole the money keeps flowing out of."

"You might not be moving after all."

He stopped in front of the porch he'd been pacing on, only an hour ago.. "Would you be sad if I didn't move to Boston?"

I wanted to tell him that what he did or didn't do had no impact on my life. But after the last few days, I'd be lying. Instead, I played it safe by saying, "I'd be sad if you gave up what you wanted for something someone else thought you needed."

He looked thoughtful, but said nothing, and for a few minutes we simply stood in the silence. His gaze was focused somewhere out over the lake when I asked him, "You said you wanted to show me something?"

Snapping out of whatever trance he'd been in, he turned toward me and held out his hand. "Yes, I wanted you to see this."

I wasn't sure what this he could want to show me in the business wing, but I was curious, so I let him lead me into his mega-sized office. From there, we moved farther inside and down a hallway Maria had told me on my first day held his workrooms.

The first workroom we passed was also the largest. It was my understanding that Luca would often display some of his designs in that room for buyers to come and see. In my mind that sounded more like a showroom, but I wasn't going to argue those tiny details.

Luca came to a stop at the end of the hall at the last door on the left. Once unlocked, he opened the door and pushed it wide open, motioning for me to enter first. The room was small. That was the first thing I noticed, probably because every other room was so large and over the top.

What caught my eye and held my attention was the dress stand in one of the corners. From what I could see, Luca was halfway through another dress for Gemma. My feet moved of their own accord across the floor to the stand.

"When I get stressed out, or just need to clear my head," Luca said from behind me. "I come here and work on these for Gemma."

"Does it not work the same when you design clothes for women?"

He shook his head. "The last line I designed was inspired by you."

I sucked in a breath. "I didn't know."

"I didn't announce it to the public," he said. "And so many people loved it and praised it and wanted more. But there's not anything left. I used up all my creativity on your line."

"I don't believe that for a second," I said. "I've seen your prior work, and it's gorgeous. You're probably stressed out about the move is all. I'm sure when you get settled, you'll start to design again."

"I don't think so," he said. "My heart isn't in it anymore, and without that, my designs are nothing but dresses and fabric."

"Where is your heart at?" I asked, not sure I was ready for his answer.

"You and Gemma," he said, and my own heart splintered. "The two of you hold it."

CHAPTER 22

WREN

For the next twenty-four hours, Luca stayed holed up in the office wing. The housekeeper took his meals to him, but she was the only one who even attempted to cross the threshold into that domain. Maria shook her head and said something in Italian that I couldn't make out.

When I asked her if he'd ever done anything similar before, she said only once before with the last women's line he designed. I let the discussion die after that because I was still uncertain how much she knew of my past with Luca.

Twenty-four hours after he entered his office/workshop area, he found me sitting outside on the porch with a view of the lake. He looked exhausted, but was smiling as if he were in on the world's biggest secret.

I stood up and put my arms around him. "Poor thing," I said. "You look as if you haven't slept in a week."

"That's funny," he added and then yawned. "I feel as if I haven't slept in two weeks."

"You should go to bed before you attempt to anything else." I'd heard people use the phrase, fall asleep standing up before, but until today I'd seen no one I thought it applied to.

He yawned again. "You're right. I want to talk with you, but it'd probably be better to do it when there's less of a chance for me to fall asleep while doing so." He lifted an arm and sniffed. "I should take a shower before I nap."

I assured him I wasn't going anywhere and watched as he walked toward the house.

BECAUSE I'D EXPECTED him to sleep for at least eight hours, it surprised me when he appeared in my room about four hours later. I raised an eyebrow as he walked in. But damn, if he didn't look completely refreshed and rejuvenated.

"It's unfair for you to look that good after only four hours of sleep," I said, but he just chuckled and sat down in one of the chairs in the small sitting area of the guest bedroom.

"I need to let you know what I've decided and done over the last day because it affects you, and if there will be any fallout from my actions, I want to proactively address them."

I closed the book I'd been reading, suddenly somber. "What are you talking about?"

"I discussed the company's financials with my advisors, and we have cancelled the move. At least in its current state." He paused and placed a hand on my knee. "Which means there won't be a need for an article on the Italian designer moving his company to America."

"That's okay," I said. "I can write it about why you changed your mind, or what you plan to do now that you aren't moving to Boston. Or not. It really doesn't matter."

"Why doesn't it matter?" he asked.

"Because no matter what, I've decided whatever I write will be my last piece. I never wanted to be a journalist and I've decided that if I'm not passionate about it, it has no place in my life."

"You're quitting your job?"

"Yes," I answered. It was the first time I'd ever mentioned it out loud, and it amazed me at the freedom and relief I found in doing so. "So tell me what you've decided to do."

"I'm still going to go to Boston for the launch of my new line. It's important to me. You inspired it, after all. I'm taking Gemma with me when I go because she's old enough to travel and see the world, and I want her to learn and experience that there's more to life than this estate. But after the launch, I'm coming back here, though I'll probably buy a small place in Boston. To give some stability while we're there."

"And what will you be doing that will have you and Gemma traveling between here and Boston?" I asked.

"I'm going to focus on the children's designs the way you suggested," he said.

He could have said little else that would have surprised me more. "Really?"

"Yes." His eyes sparkled with an excitement I hadn't seen whenever he'd talked about work before. "All the advisors and investors were onboard. Hearing my ideas and plans for this new line did away with any doubt they might have had regarding canceling the move."

"That's wonderful news, Luca," I said. "I'm so happy you get to do what you want and that everyone is behind you. And now Gemma won't have to move. She'll be beside herself."

"As long as she doesn't mind visiting."

"I'm sure she'll be fine going wherever with you, as long as she knows that at the end of the day this is her home." I knew he was well aware of that fact. She was his daughter, and he knew her much better than I did.

"Yes," Luca said, catching my gaze and holding it. "It all sounds like a perfect plan. And it is, except for one thing."

I frowned. "What's missing?"

"You," he said softly.

"Me?"

"You're so full of questions, *vita mia*," he said with a smile. "But none of this would be happening if it wasn't for you. And I've realized that it won't be complete if you're not part of it."

He couldn't be serious. "But Luca," I said, utterly shocked and confused. "I know nothing about fashion. How could I possibly help you?"

"Look at me," he said, taking my hands in his and facing me. "You may not know fashion, but you know people. You could help with PR and marketing. You're an awesome writer and I could use your talent with words. Say you'll at least think about it, Wren. Please, at least think about it before deciding."

It was such a crazy idea, I almost told him no based on that alone. But one look in his eyes stopped me. He was serious. Sure, it was a crazy idea, but wasn't it time for me to be a little crazy?

"Let me think about it," I said.

"Thank you. That's all I ask." He leaned over and gave me a quick kiss. "I'm going to give Gemma the news about the move."

. . .

As PROMISED, I thought about it. But the more I thought about it, the more I realized that there was one item to discuss before I could make any decision.

After dinner, and after Gemma had been tucked into bed, I walked outside and found him sitting on the dock by the lake. He looked up at me expectantly when I sat down beside him.

"I need to tell you about five years ago," I said. "How prior to spending the last few days here, I thought our time in Italy before meant nothing to you."

CHAPTER 23

WREN

Five Years Ago

THE PAST TEN days had been one long hedonistic adventure. Luca was unlike anyone I'd ever known. And truth be told, I'd wondered in the back of my head if he wasn't just a little bit too good to be true. Yet, when I looked in his eyes as he was holding me, or if our eyes caught in public as he held my hand, I'd feel foolish for ever thinking he could be less than what he appeared to be. In those moments, I'd have bet anything he was and would somehow be mine.

Before experiencing it myself, I'd have rolled my eyes if anyone had told me they believed in love at first sight. Yet from our first genuine conversation when I met him for drinks the day of my arrival, I'd been slowly, but surely been changed into a believer.

I was flying hard and fast, and Luca was right there by my side. With him, everything seemed to be more. Comedy was funnier. Food tasted better. And sex? Well, sex was out of this world.

When it became that point in the night that we were exhausted, but still refused to succumb to sleep, we'd talk in whispers. What was it, I pondered, that was so different with us? Why did sex seem sexier? Why did his touch turn me to goo like no one else's ever had?

Luca would laugh and tell me to stop analyzing, that we shouldn't question why, but be happy that we'd found each other.

"So many people never find this," he'd whispered in those still sacred moments. Then he'd turn to pull me close for a kiss and we'd realize we weren't quite as exhausted as we thought.

Though we certainly tried, there times we weren't together. Usually it was because Luca had a business call to make. He'd always apologize, which I thought was sweet, but totally unnecessary. He was an up-and-coming fashion designer, I'd tell him. Of course, I didn't expect him to be off the grid and completely unreachable. Then I'd push up on my toes to kiss him and tell him that I'd see him soon, and he'd swat my butt as he turned to leave.

We'd just repeated that routine, late in the morning on my sixth day in Italy. I felt a bit of trepidation because the time was quickly approaching for my return to the US and to say I was dreading it would be the understatement of the year.

So far, Luca and I had addressed nothing past my time here, and I hadn't brought it up. It was almost as if by mutual consent, we'd agreed that if we didn't talk about it, it wouldn't happen.

I stepped out of the elevator onto my floor. We spent most of our time in his room for several reasons. For one, his room was much nicer, being a suite and all. The second reason was everyone from my group had a room on this floor. Not that it mattered a bit what anyone thought, I just didn't want to deal with the side-eyed speculation and the not-so-whispered whispers.

Halfway to my room, a door just ahead of me opened, and Laura stepped out. Her eyes widened in surprise, and she glanced around the hall, looking for someone. Luca, I decided.

"Oh my, God, Wren," she said, still looking around as if expecting Luca to jump out from behind a doorway and shout "Boo!"

"What?" I asked.

"I've been looking for you and hoping to find you when he wasn't around."

"Luca? Why?"

"Two days ago, a group of us were in the cafe downstairs, just drinking coffee and hanging out. Trying to decide what we wanted to do for the day. Betsy and I had struck up a conversation with a group of local guys who were sitting near us."

I nodded, trying to hurry the story up or at least figure out why she felt the need to tell me about having coffee with the locals.

"You and Luca walk by," Laura continued. "Neither one of you saw us, but the local guys most certainly saw you."

She pressed her lips together.

"And?" I asked.

"They started talking about Luca being a big time player, and how from the looks of it, he'd found himself a toy." She was clearly upset as she continued talking. "I asked them what they meant, and they said he liked naïve American girls and was looking for one to pave his way to America."

I didn't know how to respond. That didn't sound like the Luca I knew at all. But Laura wasn't finished.

"Then they said that he's practically engaged to a childhood friend and everyone thinks he's using you as a last fling before settling down."

I wrinkled my forehead. "That doesn't make sense. Either he's looking for an easy way to get into America or one last fling. It can't be both."

"But don't you get it? It's probably one of them, and neither of the two are good."

She truly looked worried, and I can't lie, it shocked me. I wouldn't have thought she'd care one way or the other what happened to me.

I also didn't know how to respond. If I told her the truth, that Luca wasn't using me to get into the States or as a last fling, she wouldn't believe me, and she'd probably think I wasn't taking her seriously. But I didn't want to say anything implying he was guilty, either.

"Thank you for telling me what you heard," I said, choosing my words carefully. "I truly appreciate that you're looking out for me. I promise to look into both claims and speak to Luca if necessary."

Laura nodded. "I hope it's neither one, and Luca turns out to be the great guy you think he is. The two of you looked like you were happy together."

"Thank you," I said, smiling. "We have been."

"You're welcome." She gave me a quick hug. "Sorry I have to scurry off, but I'm already late for brunch."

I told her I'd see her soon and continued into my room, but once inside I forgot what I needed out of it. Laura's words repeated inside my head. And there in the quiet and solitary space of my room, I asked myself if there was any possible way for any of what she said to be true.

Her first accusation, that he was using me to get into the US quicker, didn't make sense. Luca was a business man from a well off family. Surely if he wanted to spend an extended amount of time in the US, there were better ways to go about doing so than seducing unsuspecting American women.

As for the suggestion he was using me as one last fling, I supposed it could be possible, but it seemed so out of character for Luca. Or at least out of character for the man I thought he was. Was it possible he was playing me?

I hated Laura for suggesting it, and I hated myself for doubting Luca. Hated that for at least the foreseeable future, whenever I looked at him, a part of me would wonder if he had someone waiting for him outside the resort.

And I really hated that I couldn't remember what I came to my room for in the first place.

Luca mentioned before I left that his call shouldn't last more than an hour. He suggested we meet on the hotel's fifth floor, where they had a long wall of windows looking out over the slopes. There were numerous sitting areas and out of the way places a person could sit undisturbed. Since I couldn't think of what else I needed to do, I might as well go on up and wait for Luca.

Usually, this time of the day, there were very few people along the fifth-floor window walk. I wasn't aware of anything special being announced for that day, but for whatever reason, the floor was more crowded than usual. I worked my way through the crowds, finally finding an empty area near the end of the walk.

Once I sat down, I found that not only was it practically empty, but it provided an excellent view of the entryway. Sitting here, I'd be able to spot Luca the second he arrived. I wondered if he'd look any different to me after hearing Laura's rumors?

I glanced at my watch. Based on what he'd said, I still had about twenty minutes until he would arrive. I settled back into my seat and prepared to people watch. After several entertaining minutes of side-eyeing a bickering couple, I realized there were voices coming from behind what I assumed was a solid wall. Upon looking at it closer, I realized it wasn't a wall at all, but a pocket door.

A very thin pocket door, based on how much of the conversation being held on the other side that I could hear. Although it helped that the people involved weren't trying to be quiet or discreet. I was probably being nosey, but in my mind it was being a diligent journalist. No matter which view you took, however, the result was the same, I listened in.

Perhaps, looking back, I got what I deserved. After all, if you're going to listen in on conversations you haven't been invited to participate in, you have no right to protest the topic.

As I listened, it seemed one voice belonged to Luca.

I tried to convince myself it couldn't be Luca because Luca was back in his room on the phone for another fifteen minutes. But I couldn't do it because it sounded so much like him.

Finally, unable to stand not knowing, I walked to the edge of the door, partially obscured by a curtain, and saw a tiny crack where the door wasn't closed completely. Knowing there was no way I could stop, I peeked through the crack.

What I saw appeared to be another entrance onto the fifth floor. Odds were it was a private entrance because there were only two people standing there. Luca and a gorgeous Italian woman, who looked a few years younger than him. From the way they stood, her with her hands on her hips, and Luca with his arms crossed, they were arguing.

I couldn't have moved if the hotel had been on fire.

"I've been with you how many years?" the woman asked. "And now this? An American tourist?"

"You're being ridiculous," Luca replied. "It's nothing."

Nothing.

I wanted to crawl in a hole and die.

Nothing.

"Don't patronize me like I'm a child," she shot back. "I know what I saw."

"Stop taking this personally," Luca said.

"How else am I supposed to take it?"

"I've already told you, it's over between her and I."

And there it was again in case the it's nothing hadn't been enough. Now I'd heard it clearly spoken, Luca wanted nothing beyond my time here. In his mind, we were already finished. I'd thought it was odd that he suggested meeting here, and after hearing him talk, I knew why. He'd planned to break up with me here. He probably knew how crowded the fifth floor would be and thought that if he did it here, I wouldn't make a scene.

Feeling sick to my stomach, I moved to turn. Doing so must have shifted a light or shadows because the woman's eyes flickered my way, I froze, and for a second our gazes locked. She looked away before Luca realized anything.

I've never known what, if anything, was said next because I backed away from the door, and walked back down the fifth floor to my room.

Everything that happened next was a blur. Later, I would remember snippets and a few images, but I've never known the complete story.

CHAPTER 24

WREN

THE FOLLOWING DAY, I took my laptop with me to the estate's large outdoor area. It was too quiet inside. Maria had taken Gemma to a friend's house for the day, and Luca had a meeting in Milan. I needed to sort out my thoughts following the conversation with Luca yesterday.

After I told him everything I remembered, he'd taken me in arms. He said nothing, but he didn't have to. I'd figured out my gross misunderstanding of the conversation I'd overheard. Luca and whoever he'd been talking with hadn't been discussing me.

I hated that I couldn't remember anything substantial after that. In my mind, I saw myself talking with the same woman who'd been with Luca behind the pocket door. But I wasn't sure if it really happened or if my brain had conjured it up.

Maybe I'd never know the complete details of what happened. But that was my past, and I learned that was where it needed to remain.

However, the same wasn't true for me. I could remain in the past, even though I didn't belong there, or I could reach for the future. A future that included Luca. I attempted to create a list of pros and cons, but didn't get very far.

I was young and single, with plans to resign from my current job. There was no reason to turn down Luca's offer. Even if things didn't work out with me and Luca, the experience was priceless.

I deleted my list of pros and cons, and had just started a text to inform Luca I was accepting his offer when I heard footsteps, followed by the sound of, Stella, the estate's housekeeper.

"Ms. Carmella," Stella said. "You're not supposed to leave the office wing. This part of the estate is for family only."

I looked up to find a young woman wearing a suit storming down the path from the office wing. Behind her Stella hurried to catch up, all the while talking. "I told you Mr. Botticelli isn't here."

"I'm not here to see him." The woman was closer now and for some reason, she looked and sounded familiar.

She was also headed straight toward me.

I wasn't able to see her clearly because she wore an enormous pair of sunglasses, and though I tried, I wasn't able to place her voice. I stood to my feet, right as she walked up.

"Oh my, God," she said. "It's you."

She took her sunglasses off, and I sucked in a breath. "You."

The woman Luca had been talking with behind the pocket door.

All at once, a memory buried for years surfaces.

IT'S FIVE YEARS AGO, and I'm at the hotel bar. I'm beyond the tipsy stage, but I've done nothing stupid yet. I can tell because I'm standing.

"He's practically engaged to my best friend." The woman standing next to me is talking about Luca, and I'm believing every line she feeds me because it all seems to match what I overheard earlier in the day on the fifth floor. "He told me he was coming here to do business. Your name isn't Business, is it?"

She laughs as if she just cracked the funniest joke, ever.

I keep silent, hoping if I don't react, maybe she'll go bother someone else.

No such luck.

"Maybe he's using you to get to America." She thinks for a second and nods. *"That's got to be it. No way would he be with you by choice."*

The scene fades away.

"You CERTAINLY LOOK DIFFERENT. What the hell are you doing here?" she asked me as I blinked away the remnants of the memory.

"Fucking Luca," I said, because I knew I was looking at the person responsible for my accident. "Of course."

"I knew something was up when he let it slip an American journalist was staying here." She narrowed her eyes. "Are you the reason he canceled the move?"

"I don't see how that could be any of your business."

"His business is my job. I'm his PA."

"Then why aren't with him?" The fact that she refused to tell me led me to believe he'd sent her away. The thought made me smile. "That's okay. You don't have to tell me, the reasons I'll come up with in my head are funnier than real life, anyway."

My indifference seemed to stoke her anger. "I don't care how many times you fuck Luca, you'll always be low class American trash."

I almost laughed in her face. Had I allowed her to intimidate me so easily five years ago? It seemed I had, and Carmella was under the assumption I was the same weak thing she'd broken once before. And though she had been correct in saying I looked different, looks weren't the only things that had changed about me. She couldn't see those changes because they weren't visible on the outside, but I knew they were there, inside, and if Carmella was around me for any length of time, she'd see it. Just like Luca had when I'd turned and left his room that first night. The old Wren would never have done such a thing, the new one couldn't imagine doing it any other way.

"Carmella!"

We both whipped around at the sound of Luca's voice. He walked the same path his PA had taken moments before.

"Tell me I did not hear you disrespect a guest in my house." His eyes blazed as he came to a stop in front of us.

"Mr. Botticelli," Carmella said. "I didn't know you were there."

"Obviously." He spoke with no emotion. I'd never seen his face void of anything. "Since you appear unable to see to the needs of my guests and because I can't trust you not to say something that would disrespect whomever you're talking to, you can pack up your things here and leave. Someone will ship your personal items from the Milan office. I no longer require your services."

"You're firing me?"

"Appears that way, yes."

Carmella shot me one last nasty look before turning and stomping back up the path to the office.

Luca took out his phone and punched a button. "Jorge," he said. "Carmella will be in the office wing momentarily. Please escort her to her desk and ensure she only takes what belongs to her."

They spoke a few minutes more, and when he put his phone away, he was smiling. "That's one less thing to worry about."

I shared with him the memory that had resurfaced. He listened, growing angrier with each passing second.

"I should have gotten rid of her years ago." He shook his head. "I've known for some time now that I needed to let her go. I think I kept putting it off because somehow it felt as if I should keep her employed because of Gianna."

"Does she come and see Gemma?" I asked.

"Carmella?" He laughed. "Hell, no. She doesn't even like kids."

CHAPTER 25

WREN

"Who even are you?" Mia asked when I called to tell her everything that happened, but more importantly, the decision I'd made. "I need you to give the phone back to Wren."

I laughed. It seemed I was doing a lot of that lately. It felt good. I'd gone too many years without laughing nearly enough, and I swore right then and there it'd never happen again.

"Are you being completely serious?" Mia asked for what felt like the hundredth time.

It had been two days since Luca fired Carmella. He'd been aghast when he realized what Carmella had said five years ago. He wanted to call her back into his office for the sole purpose of firing her again, and expressed his shock over how calmly I handled everything. Especially once a few more flashbacks of that time had made their way to the surface. Somehow, seeing Carmella again had triggered something.

As I'd told him, Carmella may have lied to me, but she wasn't the one who continued to drink in my hotel room after the bar cut me off. She wasn't the one who woke up and didn't realize just how intoxicated she was, and decided to go skiing.

"Yes," I replied to Mia. "Some of my memories of the accident are coming back to me."

"Are you okay?" she asked. "Do you need to see someone and talk it out?"

I looked to my right where Luca was having a tea party with Gemma. "I'm more than okay."

Though his daughter wasn't aware, I could tell his attention was divided. And that he was listening intently to my half of the conversation.

Mia's silence sounded loud in my ears, and I could tell she didn't believe me.

"Remember what you told me before any of this happened?" I asked her.

"That I spent too much time with Tenor," she said. "And I'll have you know that is not the case because I've discovered that it's impossible to spend too much time with the one you love."

If she'd told me that two months ago, I'd have rolled my eyes and made comments about how they really needed to calm themselves down. Now, it made me smile.

"No," I told her. "You mentioned that I matched better with Luca than any other woman in the database."

"I remember."

"With that being the case, do you think there's a need to move slow?" I asked. "After all, it is your system. Don't you trust it? Because if you don't, I'm not sure you should be selling it."

Luca covered his snort with a cough.

"You okay, papa?" Gemma asked, pouring him more tea. "I don't want bad germs on my princess table."

"I'm perfectly fine, *tesoro*. Just a little throat tickle."

"Damn, I think my ovaries just exploded listening to that," Mia said with a sigh.

I had to admit, watching father and daughter play tea was quickly becoming a favorite to watch. Luca lifted his tea cup to his lips and took a sip of the pretend tea. Damn, how was it he managed to slay me no matter what he did.

"Okay," Mia said. "When you bring up how awesome my system is, I can see your point. But where are you going to live? What are you going to be doing and when will I get to see you again?"

"We're going to come to Boson in a week or so, and we're bringing Gemma." Now that she understood there wasn't a move happening, she was excited about seeing Boston. "But we don't stay forever, right? We visit and come back here."

It took her asking about twenty times before she realized the answer we gave wasn't changing.

"In a week or so..." I heard papers shuffle as she looked for her calendar on top of her desk. I never understood why she didn't use an electronic one. "Oh, this reminds me, Tenor wants to discuss someone he's been thinking about hiring with Luca. Brigitta something I can't remember. She listed him as a reference."

"I'll be sure to let him know."

We talked for a few more minutes, agreeing to get together as often as possible while I was in town. We even hinted at the possibility of Mia and Tenor coming to the estate for a visit.

"We'll definitely consider it," Mia said. "Tenor needs a vacay in the worst way. I don't think he's had one in five years."

"And when was the last vacation you took?" I asked her, knowing it had been close to five years.

"I never said I didn't need one. I'd leave tomorrow if I could. Hold on a second..." It sounded like she put her hand over the speaker instead of using the mute button. I heard conversations in the background, but I couldn't make out any of the words being said. "Wren, I hate to cut this short, but Piers is out in the lobby and Tenor still isn't talking to him so I have to handle it."

I wasn't sure what went down between Tenor and his used to be best friend, but I knew from Mia that whatever it was, still hadn't been fixed. I couldn't imagine what it would feel like to lose Mia as a friend. Whatever had happened must have been bad.

"Everything okay in Boston?" Luca asked when we'd disconnected.

I sat down beside him at the tea party table, and Gemma ran around trying to find another setting of dishes for me.

"Sounds like not much has changed." I mentioned to him what Mia had said about Brigitta, and he just nodded and said he'd answer any question Tenor had.

Realizing we'd both been left abandoned at the tea party, we glanced around the room to see what she'd gotten into. She was pressed up against the window, watching something.

"What is it, *tesoro*?" Luca asked.

"It's Auntie Maria," she said in wonder. "And she's so pretty."

Neither one of us got up to see, having ran across her earlier in the day. She'd finally agreed to go out with the man from Como who had been interested in her for so long. Apparently, she said, being around a couple had shown her what she was missing, and she needed to stop being scared and just live her life.

I leaned over and gave Luca a kiss, thinking I couldn't have said it better myself.

EPILOGUE

WREN

Two Months Later

Boston

The last two months had been the happiest of my life. Luca and I were working on building both our lives together and the new business. We've been in Boston for three days, and it's only our second trip. Gemma came with us, like she did on our first trip back. Now that she understands were aren't moving away from the estate, she's excited about visiting the States.

Maria had remained in Italy. Now that I was in the picture, she was starting to come into her own as a single lady. Not that we thought she'd be single for long - she spent a good deal of time in Como. My relationship with her had grown as well, and while she'd never take the place of Mia, she was becoming a good friend.

"Wren!" I heard Mia yell and I glanced over to my left to see she's waving at us from a picnic table. It was a Wednesday afternoon in late August, and Mia and Tenor were meeting us at a playground on the Esplanade.

Tenor and Luca shook hands. I doubted the two of them would become as close as Mia and I, but as long as they got along, I really didn't care. Mia told me after our last visit that Tenor told her Luca had found a personality. She'd corrected him, saying he'd found love.

I know she's right because Luca tells me the same thing every day.

Gemma squealed in delight at the sight of the playground and looked expectantly up at Luca. He chuckled and tussled her hair.

"Of course," he said. "But you have to stay in this area where we can see you."

She agreed and then took off toward a group of children who looked to be her same age. Within seconds, she was fully ensconced into the group.

Tenor asked Luca a question about a property we were scheduled to look at the following day. Apparently, it was in the same neighborhood as the place Tenor and Mia had recently made an offer on.

"How cool would it be if we were neighbors?" I asked Mia, taking a seat on a bench that allowed me to keep Gemma in my sight.

Mia was beaming. "If it gets you here more often, I'm all for it."

"I think once we get the new brand up and running, we'll be stateside more frequently."

"Good," she said, her eyes dancing as if she knew a secret. "I think Tenor is going to propose soon, and I'll need your help planning the wedding."

I wasn't surprised with her news. What surprised me was that he'd waited this long. "When do you think he's going to do it?"

"I don't know. I'm trying not to think about it so I can be surprised."

I laughed. "So how's the not thinking about it going?"

"Not very well." Mia grinned. "Actually, it was going pretty good until I had to help our new employee. She had Tenor's schedule pulled up on her screen, and I saw he had an appointment with a jeweler."

"Oh, no."

"Right?" She asked. "And what could I do at that point? I wasn't going to ask Tenor, *hey, by the way, how'd that three o'clock meeting go?*"

"You could," I told her.

"I could, but I didn't want to let him know that I knew, and I didn't want him to think any less of Brigitta, because she is a godsend."

The name sounded vaguely familiar to me, and I must have made some sort of expression, because Mia said, "The woman who gave Luca's name to Tenor as for a reference?"

I nodded, remembering. "The flight attendant?"

"Yes, and I should thank Luca. Everyone loves her."

We changed the topic of conversation then and it wasn't too long until the men wandered over to where we were sitting. Luca put his arm around my shoulder and pulled me toward him.

As I sat there, friends on one side, the man I loved on the other, and watching a little girl I didn't know existed a year ago, but couldn't imagine not having in my life now, it hit me. I was a dancer in every way that counted.

I danced by living to the music of life.

COMING SOON

MISTER IMPOSSIBLE, BACHELOR INTERNATIONAL BOOK 3

The unforgettable conclusion to New York Times bestselling author Tara Sue Me's Bachelor International series.

Piers Worthington has worked hard for everything he has. From a childhood spent on the streets of London, he's fought and toiled his way to where he is today - one of the most sought after attorneys in Boston.

A rift in his friendship with Tenor Butler concerning Bachelor International forces him to reassess the way he does business. He's vowed to Tenor he'll make it right, but keeps running into dead ends, until the day he runs into Brigitta, the childhood friend he was forced to leave behind in London so many years ago.

Brigitta's been led to believe Piers left her on purpose, and she's never forgiven him. Now that she has the means, she plans to destroy him. But as their passion sparks and she finds herself growing closer to him, she begins to waver. Unfortunately, the people who deceived her about Piers aren't going to let her ruin their plan for the complete eradication of Piers and all his business connections.

Trying to see between the half truths and complete lies, Piers and Brigitta have to trust each other not only to stop those who want them destroyed, but to find their way back to each other.

DON'T MISS

HOW IT ALL STARTED

MISTER TEMPTATION
Bachelor International, Book 1

He's a self proclaimed bastard with a double helping of lying asshole. He's also her new boss.

From the New York Times and USA Today Bestselling author of the acclaimed SUBMISSIVE Series comes the first book in a new series perfect for fans of Helena Hunting and Maya Banks.

Mia Matthews never thought much of big shot matchmaker Tenor Butler, but when she finds out he loaned her late business partner a quarter of a million dollars and no one told her, there aren't enough four letter words to describe him. She'd like nothing more than to pretend Tenor doesn't exist, but she owes him all that money, not to mention he's hot as hell.

Tenor doesn't see why it's his fault Mia didn't know about the loan. In fact, he thinks he's being very magnanimous when he offers to forgive the loan if Mia closes her own matchmaking business and works for him for five years. But as he gets closer to Mia, he realizes two things: 1) he doesn't want her as an employee and 2) she hates his guts.

When an old flame threatens them both, Mia and Tenor find themselves working together and are unable to ignore their mutual attraction. But it might be too late for these two romance experts to create their own love story.

Chapter One
Mia

I was walking down a sidewalk one day years ago, not really paying attention. My best friend, Wren, was with me and if I had to guess, we were probably talking about boys. It's an assumption we all have that the sidewalk will just be there when we step down. Unknowingly, I made that same assumption, and when my foot came down and met air instead of sidewalk, I sucked in a breath as I tripped into the unseen hole and fell to my knees.

The horrible knowledge that had twisted my stomach upon realizing that what I had counted on to always be there for me and was not, was the same thing I experienced the day my mother died.

She had not been sick. She didn't have anything wrong with her. One minute she and a friend, Opa, were headed to lunch and the next, her car flew into the median as a perfect stranger ran into her at a high speed in his attempt to get away from the pursuing police cruisers. Mom and Opa were killed instantly. The man who hit them had just robbed a gas station. For my entire life, my mother had been my sidewalk and then suddenly, she wasn't there anymore.

Two weeks after her funeral, I had a feeling the sidewalk was going to be ripped out from under me again. I sat in our lawyer's office and I knew it wasn't going to be good news based on the way everyone in the office looked at me when I walked in, eyes filled with something that looked like pity. I hated that. I didn't want their pity.

I also didn't want to be here. Lawyer meetings were about on par with doctor's appointments and they both always had the most uncomfortable waiting areas. It must be a periodical they all subscribe to: *Waiting Rooms to Lose Your Mind In.*

"Clayton," I said, when he finally sat down after his admin gave him some papers he'd asked for. He'd been acting edgy and odd since I walked in. "I promise I'm strong enough to handle whatever it is you're hesitant to tell me."

What worried me more than anything at that moment wasn't my suspicion that he was hiding something, but that whatever he had to tell me was going to be much worse than I had originally thought. I had asked a week ago for this meeting and he'd kept postponing with the excuse he didn't have all the paperwork.

"Mia," he said and then stopped as he read something in the folder he'd just received. He looked horrible. He'd always been on the pale side, but he appeared even more so today. Not to mention, his much-too-thin frame didn't help matters out.

"Spit it out, Clayton."

He took his glasses off and though I thought I'd prepared myself for whatever he was going to tell me, I hadn't. Not by a long shot. "You know it's been a rough year for the business," he said.

My mom and I were co-owners of Cross My Heart, a boutique dating agency in downtown Boston. She dealt with the numbers side and the money, while I worked my magic with the people side of the business. We didn't plan to get rich from our venture, but it paid the bills and we were two of the lucky ones who could say we loved our jobs.

Granted, the last year had been more difficult than others, simply because one of our well-known clients had been accused of inappropriately touching a female co-worker. Technically speaking, it shouldn't have affected us at all, but right before the allegations came out, he'd done some promo and advertising for us, so we were seen as guilty by association.

It had unquestionably been a rough time, but mom and I had put our heads together and worked through it. I blinked back a tear. God, I missed her. Who would I weather the next storm with?

"Yes," I told Clayton. I could not fall apart. Not right now. "Mama had told me, but she didn't make it out like it was anything major. In fact, I seem to remember her saying things were looking up recently."

"Yes, well," he said, shuffling through the papers. "The thing is, your mother took a loan and put the business up for collateral."

"What?" I asked, because there was no way he'd just said what I thought he did. "That can't be. There's no way she'd have done something like that and not tell me."

"I'm afraid she did. In fact, I helped with the terms of the deal. I told her when we were doing it that I thought she should bring you in." He shook his head, but refused to look at me. "She didn't want to and I didn't push it the way I should have because she thought she'd be able to repay it without you ever knowing. Obviously, we never expected this."

"How much was the loan for?" My body starting shaking, ever so slightly and I willed myself to stop.

Was that *guilt* I saw reflected in his expression?

"It's not only the matter of the amount, you see," he said. "It's also who the loan was made with."

I was starting to get the feeling that I wasn't *seeing* anything at all. I glared at him. "I think you better explain to me what it is you're so hesitant to talk about."

"Your mother got the loan from Tenor Butler."

He might as well have punched me in the stomach. My mouth opened and closed, but nothing came out. It was several long seconds before I managed to get out two words. "Tenor Butler?"

Oh, my God. Anyone other than him.

Clayton winced. "Yes. She went to a few banks first, but none of them were willing to loan her anything. Tenor was her last hope."

I still couldn't wrap my head around the fact that the business found itself in that much trouble, much less that my mother had to make a deal with the likes of Tenor Butler. But, whatever. I had a bit of money left over from her life insurance. It wasn't a lot, but hopefully it'd be enough to pay Tenor back. "How much did he loan her?"

Yes, there was definitely guilt now, written all over his face. *Shit.*

"I'm so sorry, Mia."

"How much, Clayton?" My heart felt as if it would pound through my chest, because somehow I knew it would be too much for the life insurance to cover. And yet, I still wasn't prepared for his next words.

"Two hundred fifty thousand."

My vision grew blurry and saliva filled my mouth. *God, please don't let me vomit in my lawyer's office.* I placed a hand on my belly in an attempt to stop whatever it was getting ready to do. "A quarter of a million dollars?"

Why? What for the love of God would she need that much money for?

He nodded his confirmation.

There was only one thing that kept me from passing out right there in the chair across from his desk, and that was the knowledge there was no way Mama could have gone through all that money.

"How much of that is available in the business account?" I was an idiot to have to ask. What sort of business owner didn't know how much money they had in the bank? I should have known what our balance was, but Mama was the money person and since her funeral, I'd been purposely putting it off. The thought of seeing her handwriting again and knowing she'd never write anything else...it had been too much. It still felt like too much.

"Umm." He started flipping through the papers on his desk. "Looks like there's about ten thousand as of yesterday morning."

Holy fuck! "You mean to tell me that my mother somehow spent almost a quarter of a million dollars on our business and I didn't have any idea?"

How was that possible? Was I that blind or was she that good at hiding? Following those two questions was the uncomfortable feeling that I didn't know her at all.

"It appears that way."

I stood up even though my legs felt like Jell-O. I placed both of my hands on Clayton's desk and then shoved them in my pockets when I saw how they were shaking, "I can't believe you knew all this and didn't tell me until now." I should be mad at mama, too, but she wasn't here and he was.

"Mia, your mother—"

"Don't give me that bullshit. There was no reason for my mother to get a loan for that much. Especially from *him*. I don't know what's going on here, but I'll get to the bottom of it eventually and when I do, I plan to find a new attorney."

Unable to be in the same room with him anymore and knowing there was nothing either of us could do to make the situation any better, I spun on my heels and stormed out of his office. I'm sure I received a good number of stares as I made my way out of the office building, but I honestly don't remember.

I'd walked to Clayton's office because it wasn't too far from Cross My Heart and I'd thought the physical activity would be beneficial for me. I supposed in some warped way, it turned out to be just that. Or, if nothing else, it allowed me an acceptable way to work out my anger toward Clayton.

Not that I could actually blame him for everything. Oh, no. That honor belonged to no one other than Tenor Butler himself. Some part of my brain tried to tell the rest of me that logically, the majority of the blame belonged to my mother. But I told that part of my brain to sit down and shut up.

Tenor Butler owned and operated the most successful dating agency in Boston, hell, probably the entire East Coast—Bachelor International. Of course, that wasn't why I didn't like him. Seriously, I'm not petty enough to be angry because someone is more successful than me.

I didn't like him because I didn't like his entire approach to dating. I'd heard about some of his practices and I thought they were cookie cutter and impersonal. To me, matchmaking was an art. Or at least a skill to master. To Tenor it wasn't anything more than a ten-page questionnaire with multiple choice answers. *Multiple choice.*

Are you kidding me with this?

But he wasn't and obviously, his way worked, because like I said, most successful agency in Boston. And yet, I didn't feel like what he did was real. Anyone could gather statics based on multiple choice answers, but they wouldn't tell you about your client's deep down wants and needs and fears.

Maybe that was it. Maybe I felt as if Tenor was getting ahead by cheating in a way. He'd somehow managed to be successful by circumventing the upfront work needed in order to properly make a match. I let that stew as I walked back.

I thought I'd actually calmed down quite a bit by the time I reached my office. Obviously, though, my countenance left something to be desired because Wren, who'd agreed to sit and watch over the office while I was gone, looked up as soon as I walked in and said, "What the hell happened to you?"

I shook my head. I wasn't really ready to talk about it, wasn't actually sure I'd ever be able to talk about it. But Wren would be the best person to initially talk to because she knew me better than anyone.

I decided to lay it on her all at once. "Mama took a loan out for a quarter of a million dollars."

Wren's jaw dropped open.

"And that's not the worst part," I said.

"No way."

"Yes, way. *Tenor Butler* gave her the loan." It didn't make me sick to my stomach to say it anymore, but my insides still fluttered a little.

Wren's face went unnaturally pale and her eyelashes fluttered for a few seconds. I actually thought she was going to pass out or something, but her color returned and she simply muttered, "Holy shit."

"Right?" I flopped into a nearby chair. Another reason to tell Wren. She knew exactly who Tenor was, so I didn't have to spend time explaining why this was such a horrible thing.

I also truly appreciated that Wren didn't ask me questions I had no answers for, like why Mama needed that much money and where it had all gone. Why the hell Tenor Butler of all people? I'd have to ask those same questions soon enough, but I wasn't ready just yet.

"Tenor Butler," Wren mumbled and then her head shot up and she looked at me with determination in her eyes. "We need to come up with a plan on how you're going to deal with him."

I nodded. A plan was exactly what I needed. "He has to know she passed away."

Of course he would. Any good business person would know such details about someone who owed them money. Especially that much money. He more than likely knew I was her only living relative. I dug my nails into the palm of my hands, not wanting to think about being alone right now.

I couldn't help but wonder if he had any idea at all about what I thought of him and his multiple choice, cookie cutter business. Probably not.

"Yes, and my guess is he's giving you time to grieve before he approaches you," Wren added.

"I'm sure." For some reason that irritated me and I couldn't figure out why. If he'd come by and tried to talk to me the day after her funeral or something, I'd have been justified in my anger toward him. So why was I mad he was giving me space?

"I'll tell you what I'm *not* going to do," I said. "I'm not going to sit here and wait for Mr. High and Mighty Butler to summon me to his chrome and stainless steel high-rise office in the sky."

"What *are* you going to do?"

I smiled. "On Monday morning, bright and early, I'm going to beat him to it. I'm going to show up at his office and insist on seeing him." Today was Friday. That gave me the entire weekend to come up with a plan on what to do once I made it into his office. Surely I could think of something between now and then. Otherwise, I'd be handing all the control over to Tenor and that was not going to happen.

WALL STREET ROYALS

If you enjoyed AMERICAN ASSHOLE, you may enjoy...

THE WALL STREET ROYALS

Conquer. Control. Command. They have. They are. They will. They are the Wall Street Royals, men at the top of their game who are about to be mastered by the one thing they never counted on: love.

Don't miss this seductively sexy new series by New York Times bestselling author Tara Sue Me.

"...so damn HOT and intense, what an amazing start to a series..."

-The Sassy Nerd Review on FOK

ABOUT THE AUTHOR

Even though she graduated with a degree in science, Tara knew she'd never be happy doing anything other than writing. Specifically, writing love stories.

She started with a racy BDSM story and found she was not quite prepared for the unforeseen impact it would have. Nonetheless, she continued and The Submissive Series novels would go on to be both New York Times and USA Today Bestsellers. One of those, THE MASTER, was a 2017 RITA finalist for Best Erotic Romance. Well over one million copies of her books have been sold worldwide.